THE
HOCUS-POCUS
DILEMMA

E.S.Pecially for Elizabeth!
Your friend,
Pat Kibbe
5/8/86

**Other APPLE® PAPERBACKS
You Will Want to Read:**

THE HOCUS-POCUS DILEMMA

By
PAT KIBBE

Illustrations by
Dan Jones

AN
APPLE ®
PAPERBACK

SCHOLASTIC INC.
New York Toronto London Auckland Sydney

For my wonderful family

ISBN 0-590-30093-8

12 11 10 9 8 7 6 5 4 3   5 6/8
                    Printed in the U.S.A.   11

Contents

A Christmas Card

That's me with the hair ribbons and ponytails, holding one corner of the Joy to the World sign my older sister, Allison, made for this year's Christmas card. She's the one with the bangs and the stupid smile holding the other corner. The boy behind me, dangling the two gerbils over my shoulder, is Ethan. His hair always looks like that because he has a cowlick. He's my youngest brother. If you look real hard, you can find my oldest brother, Kyle. It's his head sticking through the wreath that's over the middle of the sign. He's sixteen and has a driver's license. Actually, he's very tall. He looks short because he's on his knees. The one standing next to Allison, who looks like he has the mumps, is my brother Jon. He's just eating something. He's always eating something.

Mom can't get Dad to pose for the Christmas cards, ever. I think it's because he's losing his

1

hair. And she always says she can't be on it without him, so that's why you can't find them.

That fuzzy ball on the floor near Jon's left foot is Willie, our dog. If you look real close, you can see the hole he bit in the armchair I'm leaning on. He gets excited when the phone rings and bites things if no one is around to answer.

Allison tried to get Love on the card, too. But Mom wouldn't let her. "A house is no place for a horse," Mom said.

Mr. Buckingham took this picture December 3. I'm surprised it even came out, because in the newspaper my horoscope said it was "a bad day for developments." It was right about Ethan, though. His horoscope said, "Your problems will multiply." As soon as Mr. Buckingham snapped the picture, one of Ethan's gerbils got loose. (We still can't find it.) The other one had five babies that night.

B.J.

P.S. The J stands for Justine. I tell everybody the B stands for Barbara. I'd die before I'd tell the truth. Who wants to be called Baby Justine when you're almost ten, for heaven's sake? I was going to change the *B*, but Nancy Tyler— she's my best friend—says that's good luck. In her fortune-telling book, under "Ancient Divination by Letters of the Alphabet," the letter *B* denotes a person who comes to the rescue of others in unfortunate circumstances. The letter *J* is "a favorable sign indicating the person has insight and the ability to look beyond what seems to be."

Nancy says that means I'm gifted and should be a fortune-teller. I thought she was kidding me, but then, one day, I discovered I had extrasensory perception — E.S.P.

On December 20, the phone rang. Before anyone could answer it, I said, "That's Uncle Dave calling long-distance." And it was! That's when I knew I had E.S.P. And that's when I began thinking about going into the fortune-telling business. I told Mom the only thing I wanted for Christmas was... a crystal ball.

The Magic Circle

For Christmas I got a bicycle from Mom and Dad, some playing cards I'd asked Kyle to give me, a window thermometer from Jon, and a baby gerbil from Ethan. Allison gave me a book about horses. Aunt Maud sent money. Best of all, Nancy Tyler gave me her old fortune-telling book and a new one on E.S.P.

I sent away to a magic shop in New York City for my crystal ball. I didn't dare tell Mom I'd spent Aunt Maud's five dollars on it. She'd have a fit. But I knew I'd make it back as soon as my fortune-telling business got started.

I'd finished my sign and taped it to the outside of my bedroom door.

4

Come and meet the Spirits
at the Gypsy Caravan
Crystal Gazing
Fortune-Telling
Palm Reading
We will analyze your handwriting
Open 3 P.M. to 10:30 P.M.
Please stay out unless teller is in... or else!

The playing cards Nancy and I had glued on the sign looked great. I went into my bedroom and closed the door. After I pulled down the shades, I took my crystal ball out of the secret hiding place. (I'm not allowed to tell even Nancy where I hide it, or let anyone touch it. It breaks the power.) I let down the curtains I had tacked to my canopy bed and climbed in.

First I had to make the Golden Magic Circle. I peeked at page 31 of my E.S.P. book. It said, "Visualize a golden circle all around you." I closed my eyes and did it. Then I peeked again. "If you happen to be in danger, upset, or discouraged, you should remember your magic circle is completely surrounding you." That was good to know. Now I had to begin breathing very deeply and slowly to enter the Sacred Inner Silence. I was supposed to meditate to develop my E.S.P. abilities. I closed my eyes and let my mind wander.

I don't know why, but I kept thinking about

my brother Kyle and that Beth Shepherd. Beth Shepherd was pretty, but other than that I couldn't imagine what Kyle saw in her. She had Kyle wrapped around her little finger. I mean, he'd do anything for Beth. When her club decided to raise money by selling chances for a raffle, who do you think bought ten chances, at a dollar apiece, and is in debt for probably the rest of his life? You're right! Kyle. I hated to see Kyle being taken advantage of, but Mom says he's just naturally nice to everyone, and I shouldn't worry. It's a good trait.

"Hey, B.J."

I popped out of my trance. "Who calls?"

"It's me, Kyle."

Wouldn't you know! "Enter."

"Hey, this is terrific, B.J. Where'd you get all the half-moons and stars?"

"Oh, Nancy and I cut them out and pasted them around. Want your fortune told?"

"Well—"

"It's free, just for practice. Come into my booth."

Kyle pushed aside a curtain and sat on the bed.

"First, I'll read your palm." I took Kyle's hand. "See, that's your life line, there near your thumb. Hey, you're gonna live forever.

These two lines below your fingers going across your palm are the head—boy, are you intelligent!—the other's your heart. Oh, oh, your love life's all cracked up, Kyle."

Kyle laughed.

"Now I'll look into my crystal ball. See, it's getting all cloudy. Wait! Wait! It's clearing up. I see... I see... I see you are going to take a voyage, a long, exciting voyage."

Kyle laughed again. "B.J., you're too much."

"Wait till you hear your fortune with the cards, Kyle."

"Thanks, but that's enough, B.J."

"Please, Kyle, wait," I begged. I grabbed the fortune-telling book and the cards from under my pillow and shuffled three times. That makes it work. "Just draw any five cards."

"O.K., but make it quick." Kyle drew five cards and handed them back to me, facedown.

I placed them faceup on the bed—

> King of Clubs
> Queen of Diamonds
> Jack of Clubs
> Ten of Hearts
> King of Spades

I opened my book and read out loud. " 'King of Clubs: a humane person, upright and affectionate, faithful in all his undertakings, tries to make others happy.' " That sounded just like Kyle!

" 'The Queen of Diamonds: a flirt, a fickle and unfaithful person. The Jack of Clubs: an open, sincere, and good friend, who will exert himself warmly in your behalf. The King of Spades: an ambitions man, envious, ruthless, but successful in love matters.' "

"Oh, B.J., I've had enough." Kyle was laughing his head off.

"Wait, I haven't finished." I was getting angry. "I haven't done the Ten of Hearts."

"Forget it. I have to go, B.J. Thanks anyway." Kyle jumped off the bed. I could hear him, still laughing, as he went down the back stairs.

I decided I'd have to memorize what each card meant. Then I could go faster. So I spent all Friday doing just that.

Saturday morning Kyle was practicing on his drums. I was in his room making his bed just so I could listen. He really can play on those drums.

"Will you stop that racket?" Allison ran by and slammed the door.

Kyle's music was always pretty loud, especially with the cymbals and that foot pedal for the extra drum. Even with the door closed though, I heard the phone ringing. Someone answered because it stopped ringing and Willie stopped barking.

"It's for you, Kyle," Mom called.

"I'll get it on the upstairs extension," Kyle called back and started out the door.

"It's Beth Shepherd, Kyle," I said.

"Sure, B.J." He winked at me and went into Mom and Dad's bedroom to answer the phone.

I pulled up the bedspread wondering what had got into my head. I mean, that I should say it was Beth Shepherd.

Kyle came back. "You're pretty good at that E.S.P. stuff," he told me. "It *was* Beth Shepherd. She can't go out tonight because she has relatives visiting for the weekend." He picked up his drumsticks.

"Too bad." I really thought he was being blessed and didn't know it.

The phone rang again. Willie barked.

"It's for you, B.J.," Mom called.

Kyle clashes the cymbals. "I have a ghastly vision," he said. "It's Nancy Tyler."

I giggled and went to answer. What a sense of humor that Kyle has.

"Getting it up here, Mom." I lifted the receiver. "Hello, this is B.J."

"Hello, B.J.? It's Nancy. Can you go to the movies tonight?"

"I don't know, Nancy. Why, can you?"

"Uh-uh. My mother says I can go if we can get a grown-up or somebody older to sit with us."

"I've got it. Kyle's not busy. Beth Shepherd's having company for the weekend, so Kyle can take us instead." I held my hand over the mouthpiece and shouted. "Kyle! Kyle, will you take Nancy Tyler and me to the movies tonight?"

"Ah-hah! So it was Nancy Tyler, huh? What's playing and how much do I get for baby-sitting?" Kyle did a roll on his drums.

"I hear it's a real scary science fiction with no mush. Come on, Kyle. Please."

"Aw, O.K. But Mom will have to drop us. You know I can't drive after eight o'clock."

I took my hand off the mouthpiece. "Nancy. Nan, if I don't call back that means everything is all set. We'll pick you up at seven thirty."

The Park Theater is always crowded Saturday nights, so Nancy and I went into the waiting section of the lobby to get some popcorn while Kyle got in line to buy the tickets.

"Put some extra butter on it," I said to the fellow behind the popcorn machine.

"That'll be ten cents more." He handed me two bags.

10

"I'll get it, B.J." Kyle walked up and paid for it. Nancy and I felt wonderful.

We followed him into the main part of the theater. The movie had already started. I couldn't see a thing. But there was Kyle's best friend, Eddie Dowling, the head usher, all dressed up in his uniform.

"Hey, what are you doing here, Kyle?"

"I have a date with B.J. and Nancy Tyler," Kyle said. We both giggled. That Kyle sure is funny. "Any seats left?"

Eddie hesitated and started brushing off the brass buttons on his uniform. Then he looked straight at Kyle and said, "Sure, sure. Boy, have I got seats for you."

Before I knew it, we were following his flashlight down the center aisle to about the middle, where he pointed to three seats.

I opened my bag of popcorn and Nancy and I started eating. It was pretty good popcorn, but the movie was terrible. They made it out to be so thrilling in the ads, but all it was, was another stupid love story, so I concentrated on my popcorn. I offered some to Kyle, but he didn't want any. I kept wishing those silly people in front of us would stop being so lovey-dovey. They were so close to each other I couldn't see the movie even if I wanted to.

I turned to say something about them to

Kyle. That's when I realized who the girl was. It was Beth Shepherd! What a fickle person. Then I remembered! Of course, the Queen of Diamonds, "a flirt, a fickle and unfaithful person." And Eddie Dowling, he was the Jack of Clubs, that "open, sincere, and good friend, who will exert himself warmly" in Kyle's behalf.

Kyle already knew. I could tell, even in the dark. That certainly wasn't the movie he was watching. And that certainly was no relative with Beth, either. It was the King of Spades, Philo Milton, "ambitious...ruthless, but successful in love matters."

I thought the movie would never end. When it did, and the lights went on, you should have seen Beth Shepherd's face when she saw Kyle and knew he had been sitting behind her all the time.

"Hello, K-Kyle," she stammered.

"Hi there, Kyle." What a face that Philo Milton had!

"Come on, B.J., let's get out of here," Kyle muttered, and we left.

"She's only with Philo because he's got a senior driver's license." I tried to make Kyle feel better.

"Want some popcorn?"

Luckily, Mom was waiting with the car right

outside. We hopped in, dropped Nancy off, and went home.

I felt so awful that I couldn't even be glad about being such a good fortune-teller.

The next morning, I knocked on Kyle's bedroom door. I still hadn't told him what the other card, the Ten of Hearts, meant. I knew he'd feel better when I told him.

The phone rang. Willie barked.

"For you, Kyle," Mom called up the stairs.

As Kyle ran past me, I squeezed my eyes closed. Using all the E.S.P. I could, I said, "It's Beth Shepherd. She's calling to apologize for last night."

"Forget it, will you, B.J." Kyle looked so mad I thought he was going to hit me. Instead he went into Mom and Dad's room to pick up the extension.

I waited in the hall till he came back.

"Well, what did Beth say?" I asked as he went by me on his way downstairs.

"Nothing."

"How come?"

"It wasn't Beth. That's how come."

"Oh." My E.S.P. had failed. "Who was it?"

"Marsha Lane."

I didn't know much about Marsha Lane except that she was president of that club Beth Shepherd belonged to. But Kyle was running down the stairs and out the back door. I had to tell him about the Ten of Hearts.

I dashed into my bedoom and pushed up the window. It had just started to snow and Kyle was headed out the driveway.

"Wait a minute, Kyle! I forgot to tell you about the Ten of Hearts. It means everything is going to work out fine, no matter what."

Kyle turned around and walked back toward the house. He stopped under my window and looked up. "You know, you're quite a fortune-teller, B.J."

I thought he was making fun of me. I started to close the window.

"No, really," he said, "and I'm surprised you don't know where I'm going."

"Where?"

"To Marsha Lane's house to pick up the tickets."

"Tickets? What tickets?"

"The tickets for my voyage."

"Voyage? What voyage?"

"You remember—the long, exciting voyage you told me I'm going on. I'm going to pick up the cruise tickets. I won the raffle." Kyle grinned. Then he turned and ran down the driveway.

I poked my head farther out the window and

watched as he passed the driveway gates and disappeared around the corner.

I shivered, but not from the cold. It was the sudden realization that what Nancy Tyler had said was true. I *was* gifted. I had a magical power. I brushed a snowflake off my nose and closed the window. I jumped back on my bed so hard I almost bounced up to the canopy. I was gifted!

Abracadabra

Dad's a lawyer, so he's the practical one in the family. He convinced Kyle to sell his cruise tickets and put the money away for college. I told Kyle I could have gone on that cruise with him and made enough money for his tuition by reading everyone's fortune.

"You're still too much of a novice, B.J.," Kyle replied.

"What's that mean?"

"It means you don't know enough about what you're trying to do," butted in Jon.

"You have to work and practice for years, like a ballerina." Allison did a crazy twirl and landed upside down on the sofa.

"That's not true, stupid," said Ethan. "I heard of someone who fell off a thirty-foot ladder on his head and immediately became a clairvoyant. You could do that, B.J."

"A what?"

"A clairvoyant," repeated Ethan.

"That means you know what other people are thinking and doing before they do," explained Jon.

I didn't feel much like falling off a thirty-foot ladder, but I did want to develop my fortune-telling talents.

I told Allison I needed some money to put down on a birthday present for her. So she loaned me some of her baby-sitting money. I used it to send away for books listed on the back of my fortune-telling book.

"It is of utmost importance that you develop your mental powers secretly," warned my E.S.P. book. When *Abracadabra, the Cure for Evil Spirits* arrived, I hid it under my mattress. I borrowed Ethan's flashlight so I could study in bed when everyone else was sleeping.

One night about a month later, while I was reading, Ethan ran past my bedroom door and bounded down the back stairs. I nearly fell out of bed I was so startled.

"There's something in the trap. There's something in the trap," he shouted.

"Wait for me," I yelled. I ran after him in my pajamas.

"All right, but for heaven's sake, don't let Willie out. And bring that flashlight of mine you took," Ethan shouted back at me and flew out the kitchen door.

It was dark and kind of scary, but I followed Ethan. I wished that Willie would get out, in spite of what Ethan said. Not that Willie, who was snoozing away in his basket under Mom and Dad's bed, is much protection — but he sounds fierce. And I'd just been reading that animals are very good at scaring away evil spirits.

I handed Ethan his flashlight. The beam bounced across the grass, over to the pine trees, and suddenly stopped, focusing on an object in his Havahart trap.

"Is it a raccoon, Eeth?" I whispered.

"Don't know yet, just be still, will ya, B.J., and let go of my shirt."

We crept slowly toward the clump of trees.

You see, my brother Ethan is as crazy about raccoons as my sister, Allison, is about horses. He spent a whole year's allowance on Havahart traps, hoping he would catch a raccoon.

"These are very special traps, B.J.," Ethan told me, "named after what they do. They

18

'have a heart.' They catch the animal but don't hurt it. Get it? Havahart."

I got it, but I think the name is silly. They're just plain wire cages really, only doors slide up on both ends, and when an animal walks in, the door drops. *Zip! Bang!* It's as simple as that.

Well, Ethan had these traps set all over the place, little ones and big ones, on the porch, in the garbage cans, across the driveway under the pine trees, any place that was near enough so he could watch and listen from his bedroom window.

He even wrote away and got some Raccoon Lure. Ethan knows all about things like that. He said Raccoon Lure was to a raccoon like peanut butter was to me. It sure didn't smell like it. It smelled terrible. Ethan would put it on some bread and put it in the cages, but it didn't do a thing except get Mom angry because all the kitchen knives got smelly and turned green.

All of a sudden, Willie streaked out the door and past us, barking like crazy.

"I thought I told you not to let him out," said Ethan. "He'll scare my raccoon."

We both started running after Willie, but Willie reached the trap before we could grab him. He was barking furiously. He wasn't scared, though. I could see his tail wagging as he stood in the beam of the flashlight, staring at the cage. Suddenly he stopped barking, sort of choked, and bolted back toward us. I made a grab for his collar and snatched him up, so Ethan wouldn't get even madder at me.

Whew! I dropped him twice as fast.

"It's not a raccoon, Ethan," I said.

Ethan held his nose and nodded.

"We'd better get Mom and Dad," I told him.

We started running back to the house. Ethan didn't need his flashlight now because the moon was so bright. Neither did Willie. He ran past us, through the doorway and into the kitchen.

"You'd better get Willie out of here," I practically screamed at Ethan. "He smells horrible."

Too late. Willie was already headed for the stairs. By the time we caught up with him, he was on top of Mom and Dad's bed, rolling all over their quilt, just like he does when he finds a smelly fish on the beach. But this time I don't think he liked the smell as much. He was trying to get rid of it.

I made a lunge for Willie, but he scooted off the bed and dived back into his basket.

"What's that awful smell?" Mom sat right up.

"Willie," I told her.

"Wake up, Dad," said Ethan. "Guess what?"

"What?" mumbled Dad.

"Those traps really work. I caught something."

"Good," said Dad and he turned over on his other side.

"I think — I think," Ethan stammered. "I think I caught a — a —"

"A skunk!" I shouted.

"That's nice," yawned Dad. Then he sat up and moaned, "Oh, no!" He staggered out of bed and put on his trousers.

"Oh, yes," sighed Mom, jumping out of bed. She didn't bother to dress. She yanked Willie out of his basket and started downstairs in her nightgown. Willie trotted after her, but every once in a while he'd have to sit down and wipe his nose with his paw. Mom shoved him out the door, hoping the smell would go out with him, but it didn't.

Dad and Ethan went outside to decide what to do about the skunk. Mom and I began hauling out cans of tomato juice from the kitchen cupboard. Mom read somewhere that tomato juice is about the only thing you can use to take away the smell of a skunk. We dumped the juice in a pail and carried it out on the porch. I tied Willie to the back doorknob, and Mom began scrubbing him.

"Mom, come quick! Dad needs your help. And bring the broom." It was Ethan.

Mom and I ran across the yard to the old pine tree. Dad was trying to lift the door of the trap with a long stick so the skunk could walk out.

Ethan was dancing around screaming, "Don't hurt him! Don't hurt him!"

I just stood and stared. I never in my life saw such a huge skunk. It must have been three times the size of Meowner, our barn cat. It didn't move. Not an inch. That skunk just sat there and stared right back at me.

"Give him a little shove with the broom," Dad said to Mom.

"Who, me?" said Mom. "Are you crazy?"

"Don't worry, Mom," shouted Ethan, still jumping up and down. "Once they spray, they don't spray again for a while."

"Are you sure?"

"I think so," added Ethan.

"Hurry," said Dad.

Mom took the broom and carefully walked toward the trap. The skunk still didn't budge. Mom got real close. She poked the broom into the cage. The skunk arched his back and lifted his tail.

"Watch out!" shouted Ethan.

Mom dropped the broom. Dad dropped the

stick. Ethan stopped dancing up and down, and I started to run. Then everybody ran.

"You're safe after ten feet," hollered Ethan. "That's the farthest a skunk can aim and hit its mark."

Either Ethan's information was all wrong, or we didn't run fast enough.

From a safer distance, we watched as the skunk nudged the door of the trap open, all by himself. He took one last look at us, slowly turned, and waddled back to the stone wall, where he disappeared through a hole.

It had all been too much for Willie. When we got back to the porch, he was asleep, next to an empty pail. He had drunk all the tomato juice. And he still smelled worse than anybody.

"You'll have to sleep outside for a month, Willie," Mom moaned.

"And so will we," sighed Dad.

"Don't be silly, Jack. But you'd better bury all our clothes as soon as we take a bath."

That's when I remembered *Abracadabra*. Here was a chance to use my magical powers! "Don't worry, about Willie, Mom. I've got the perfect cure. And it's not tomato juice."

After I took a bath, I secretly checked my book. I was right. It said Abracadabra was an amulet, a good-luck charm, and could make evil spirits disappear.

First, I got a little piece of paper and printed
a sign, like this:

```
A B R A C A D A B R A
 AB RA C A D A B R
 A BR A C A D AB
  AB R A C A DA
  AB R A C AD
  AB R A CA
  AB R AC
  AB RA
  ABR
  AB
  A
```

The book said the patient (Willie) would be
cured of the plague if he wore the amulet for
nine days.

I got a piece of string and tied the paper onto
Willie's collar. Sure enough, within nine days,
Willie had completely recovered. Just as the
word shrank away to nothing, so did Willie's
odor.

When I told Ethan about Abracadabra he
said, "You're crazy, B.J. It was all those bub-
ble baths and creme rinses Allison gave him
that did it."

I tried to explain. "It's called an amulet. You
wear it and it brings good luck."

To prove it, I tied Abracadabra signs on each Havahart trap.

In nine days, Ethan caught three more skunks, four stray cats, three squirrels (two gray and one red), and an oppossum.

He still wouldn't agree it was magic. "It's just springtime, B.J."

But the next day when he woke up and found he'd caught Willie, he tore off the amulets.

Abracadabra!

Friday the Thirteenth

It was a late Friday afternoon in April when Mom found the *Abracadabra* book under my mattress. She was looking for Ethan's flashlight to take on the camping trip. It was absolutely impossible to keep my talent hidden any longer. Mom said she didn't believe in all that hocus-pocus, and she didn't approve of all the literature that was arriving in the mail either, but she said she guessed it was all right as long as another failure notice from school didn't arrive with it.

"Wait and see, Mom. All this reading is bound to improve my marks." I grabbed my latest book, *Superstitions of the Ancient*

Seers, and packed it in the car with the tent and things for the trip.

The minute Dad drove out of the driveway, Mom started singing, "We are going to our mountain, we are gooooing to our mountain." She was way off key, but nobody cared. We were all feeling so good we would have joined in, but we couldn't because it was some silly song she made up as she went along.

We call it a mountain, but it's really a hill. My father says he bought it for Mom, but Ethan says he bought it because he likes to go camping. I agree with what Dad says, but then I agree with Ethan too. Dad loves Mom all right, but he sure loves camping. Anyhow, they found it when they were out driving away up in the country.

I know the story by heart because every time the family goes up there, Mom tells it. She loves it when we're her prisoners, trapped in the car, her captured audience. Kyle, Jon, Eeth, and I are always squashed into the back of the station wagon. Allison gets to sit up front with Mom and Dad — she pretends she gets car sick. Willie goes too. He loves going anywhere in the car so he can stick his nose out the window and let his ears flap away.

Mom started telling the same old story

again, about how Dad drove up this winding dirt road, and there was this lovely cleared field on the very top. Dad pulled over to the side of the road and he and Mom got out. They ran through the field and Dad grabbed Mom and kissed her. What mush! They looked at the view and Dad said, "Let's buy it."

I was glad I brought my book along. I started to read the chapter about lucky and unlucky days, while Mom rambled on.

"Hey," I interrupted her, "listen to this everybody. 'Friday is widely thought to be unfortunate for starting new projects, taking a trip and so on.'"

"Oh, oh, guess we'd better turn back, Dad," Jon said.

"And it's Friday the thirteenth, B.J. We definitely better not go on," Kyle teased.

I didn't say a word. I couldn't help seeing the sentence that followed. "If a Friday happens to fall on the thirteenth of any month, it is doubly bad."

I closed my book and tried to remember the chant that Nancy Tyler had taught me. It guaranteed to break the spell of any curse. I couldn't remember!

Mom started humming her song again and we were almost there. We stopped at the town spring to fill the big plastic water jugs.

"Rain tonight," I said and pointed to a black cloud in the east.

"Nope," said Jon. "My weather maps absolutely forecast clear weather for the whole weekend."

On the back road, we passed a few old houses and some cows, but after a couple of miles there was nothing but plowed fields and trees and trees and trees. Dad slowed down and turned off the dirt road onto a smaller one that led to our property. Mom sang even louder. Then Dad stopped the car. Jon and Ethan jumped out the back window of the station wagon and let down the bars of the old fence. The car was so loaded with camping stuff and food, it practically crawled the rest of the bumpy way. Kyle hopped out too, and the three boys raced to the top where the campsite would be, smack in the middle of Dad and Mom's field. They beat us, but Dad managed to get the car to the very top of our mountain, and pulled up at the side of the field where the woods began. Then Kyle helped him carry the tent and poles and stakes into the middle of the field.

"You and Allison carry this into the wooded area and set it up," Dad said to me as he handed us the "Portable Potty" he had bought especially for Mom. Mom can't seem to get used to camping, so Dad has to baby her a bit. She had already started clearing a kitchen area. Willie went crazy, running around, sniffing and jumping at things.

Everybody was so happy. It would have been really perfect if Nancy Tyler had been able to come, but she was home sick.

"Get the wood to start the fire," Mom called.

Ethan and Jon began hunting for sticks. I left Allison wandering in the woods and started to help Mom with dinner.

"Do you feel all right, B.J.? You look pale."

"Sure, I just wish Nancy could have come."

"Next time," Mom said.

All of a sudden Allison was running out of the woods screaming, "A bear, a big black bear!"

"Don't be silly," said Dad. "There're no bears around here."

"Oh, yes there are, Dad," Ethan spoke up. "There are over seventy-two thousand black bears in the United States, and lots have been seen in this area. Hey, will ya look?" Ethan pointed to the lower end of the field. A large black animal darted behind a bush and disappeared.

"A cub," shouted Jon. "It's a cub!"

"Yep," said Ethan. "Must be about two months old and I'll bet it just came out of the den."

Allison screamed again.

"Don't get hysterical, it's just a baby bear," said Kyle.

"But, where there's a baby, there must be a mother," Mom thought out loud.

"And a father," I added.

"Don't worry," Dad told us. "If we don't bother them, they won't bother us. Come on, it feels like rain."

"Can't rain, can't rain," muttered Jon, as a drop fell on my nose.

"Better hurry with the tent," said Mom. "And where did you pack the can opener?"

"What can opener?" asked Dad, who had been organizing everything for weeks.

"You can't open the beans without a can opener, you know," Mom replied. The neatly packed kitchen stuff was soon all over the ground. No can opener. Luckily, Ethan had his ax, so he chopped off the tops of the cans.

By then it had begun to rain, and Dad and the boys hadn't even figured out how to put the tent up, as usual.

"Hurry up," called Mom. "It's getting late

and everything's getting wet. I think that pole belongs on the other side," she said, walking over to them. "You've got them mixed up."

"You just take care of the food," Dad reminded her.

I agreed with Mom, but I didn't dare say anything.

Somehow the tent was pitched, but the poles still wiggled.

"It's the darn slate rock," Kyle explained. "You can't find any dirt to drive the stakes in. There's no dirt, just rocks."

By the time it was safe to enter the tent, it was pouring so hard the campfire had sizzled out. We all huddled inside, sitting on our sleeping bags and passing around the cold beans and raw hotdogs.

"It's Friday the thirteenth for sure," I mumbled.

"Wait until morning," Dad said as he lit the oil lamp. "It's going to be great."

I noticed Mom wasn't singing anymore. Instead she said, "Well, let's get to bed. Where's my cot?"

Dad ran to the station wagon to get it for her. The boys and Allison and I unrolled our sleeping bags while Mom got into her long underwear—otherwise she'll freeze, she says.

"Ouch," said Allison, jumping up. "There are rocks and bumps all over."

"Well, if you had done some work instead of hiding in the woods—" Kyle started.

"For Pete's sake, stop arguing," said Jon.

"And go to sleep," grumbled Ethan.

"Must have forgotten the cot." Dad poked his head into the tent. Mom didn't say anything, which is always a bad sign.

Dad put out the light, and they squeezed in someplace. With seven people on the floor of the tent there wasn't much room for Willie, but he managed to snuggle between Mom and Dad.

I couldn't get to sleep. I kept trying to remember the words of that secret chant. I knew the weekend was doomed if I couldn't think of it.

Crash! I never heard such a clap of thunder in my whole life! And then, a flash of light that lit up the entire tent. Willie bolted out the opening like a rocket.

"Catch Willie," Mom screamed. But it was too late. The noise had scared him out of his senses.

"He's probably halfway home by now," I said.

"Or eaten by that bear," screeched Allison.

"Go find him!" Mom yelled at Dad.

"Calm down!" Dad yelled back. "He'll be all right.

"If you don't go, I will." Mom stood up in her long underwear.

Dad went.

He was gone at least an hour. By then the tent was leaking buckets. Allison was moaning away, and the boys were fighting. I felt terrible. My throat was sore. I could hardly swallow. What a camping trip! I wished I was back home in my canopy bed.

It had finally stopped raining when Dad opened the flap to the tent. He practically threw Willie in. Willie was drenched. He smelled just like a wet dog smells. Mom grabbed him and put him in the sleeping bag anyway.

Dad picked up his sleeping bag and started out.

"Where do you think you're going, Jack?" asked Mom.

"I'm sleeping out on the ledge," Dad muttered, and was gone.

Then it started raining like mad again. I thought we'd be washed right off the mountain top.

In the middle of the night, I woke myself up,

mumbling. I was reciting the chant! I remembered it!

I sat up in my sleeping bag and chanted:

"Pray to the Moon when she is around.
Luck with you shall then abound.
What you seek for shall be found
In sea or sky or solid ground..."

Things were going so badly, I thought I'd better repeat it. "Pray to the Moon when she is around—"

"Go to sleep." Jon poked me.

Then I remembered what else Nancy had told me, that all spells had to be broken when the moon was full. Full? With all those clouds up there, who could even find a sliver? It was no use. I lay back and my head hit a rock. It was still Friday the thirteenth.

When I woke up again, the tent was half collapsed. Part of me was sticking outside. It was damp and drizzly. Mom was poking her head into the tent.

"Wake up, children," she said. "I can't find your father."

"Do you think he rolled off the cliff?" gasped Allison.

"You're a nut," said Ethan, but everyone started hunting for Dad.

Mom was really worried. I could tell. Her voice kept going higher and higher as she called, "Jack, Jack, where are you, Jack?"

Then we all stood still and listened, but there was nothing but an echoing "Jack, Jack," sort of bouncing off the mountain top. It was real eerie.

Jon got organized and figured out a plan. Each one of us had to search a different area. Allison and I went over near the steep edge, Ethan and Kyle took the wooded part, and Jon hiked down the dirt road a bit. Mom wandered around the field in her long underwear calling, "Jack, Jack!"

After about an hour, we met back at the camping site. There was no sign of Dad at all. Allison began wailing something about getting the sheriff, when all of a sudden, Willie started barking at the back of the station wagon.

Kyle ran over to him. "What is it, Willie?"

Willie kept barking and jumping up near the rear door.

Kyle opened it.

There was Dad, snoring away.

I didn't know whether Mom was going to hug him or hit him. Instead, she stood there and cried. My feet were squooshing inside my sneakers. We were all soaked from the high, wet grass. The bugs were biting and we were starved. Dad finally woke up — it's hard for him to wake up—well, once he did, he jumped right out of the station wagon and tried to start a fire, but the kindling was too wet.

"We can't eat the bacon and eggs raw," whined Allison.

Mom cried louder than ever, and Dad started to pack up the wagon.

"Hey, there's that bear coming up the road," yelled Ethan.

Sure enough, it was coming right at us. Allison ran back into the tent and I headed for the station wagon.

Willie, barking furiously, started toward the animal.

"Willie, come back!" Mom called.

"Hey, that's not a bear," exclaimed Kyle. "It's a dog."

"Why it's that old black mutt of Abby Whitman's. He came up to play with Willie." For the first time since we arrived, Dad smiled!

"You're some nature boy, Ethan," said Jon.

"Yeah? What about your weather predictions?" asked Ethan.

"But the sun is coming out," shouted Jon.

And it was. The mist was rising and you could see other mountains all around for miles and miles, and right over our heads, one tremendous rainbow. We all started laughing. Allison grabbed Willie and began to dance. Ethan did a flip. Jon jumped over a bush. Kyle whistled as he tightened the ten poles. And there, there was Dad kissing Mom right in the middle of their field.

I wanted to sing I was so happy. But I couldn't. My throat hurt too much. My jaws ached and my cheeks seemed swollen.

"Guess we broke that Friday the thirteenth jinx, B.J." Dad smiled at me.

I nodded as I turned up the collar of my turtle-neck sweater. This was going to be the best weekend ever, and I didn't want anyone to know I'd caught the mumps from Nancy Tyler until it was time to go home.

Written in the Stars

I got over the mumps, but I couldn't get over how my family continued to ignore my advice and make fun of me—especially Allison. When I explained to Mom that everything was written in the stars, I warned her that Taurus, Allison's sign, had extreme "spoiled brat" tendencies. She laughed and told me not to take my horoscope book too seriously.

One afternoon, as I got off the school bus, I had this strange feeling in my stomach. At first, I thought it was the Tuesday macaroni and cheese special Mrs. Perry serves in the cafeteria. Then I realized it must be a premonition! I walked slowly toward the house. Then I heard it.

"Row, row, row your boat,
Gently down the stream,"

39

The sound was coming from my sister's bed-room window upstairs.

> "Merrily, merrily, merrily, merrily,
> Life is but a dream."

I ran up the driveway and opened the back door.

"What's that?" I asked my mother as I threw my books on the kitchen counter.

"Not what's that, who's that. It's Allison," said Mom.

"What's she singing so loud for?"

"She's auditioning for the school play tomor-row."

"She has to sing?"

"Uh-huh. It's a musical comedy." Mom put the meatloaf in the oven.

"And she's going to sing that?"

"Yes."

"She sounds terrible."

"It's the one song she thinks she can stay on key with."

"She *thinks* is right."

"Now, B.J., be nice. You should be glad your sister has the initiative to do things like that."

I ran upstairs and into my bedroom. I couldn't believe it — that anyone could sound that bad. Thank goodness the audition was tomorrow and I wouldn't have to suffer any longer. I didn't have to gaze into my crystal ball or check her horoscope. I knew she'd never get a part, not with that voice!

After dinner she started again, and went on and on and on, until at least ten o'clock. She began to get hoarse, and the boys threatened to throw her out the window, so she went to bed.

After school the next day, the boys and I were in the kitchen with Mom, sampling some brownies. Allison came screaming up the driveway.

"I got a part! I got a part!"

I was dumbfounded. I should have checked my horoscope book.

"Wonderful, Allison!" Mom hugged her.

"You're kidding," said Ethan.

"Doing what?" asked Jon, grabbing the last two brownies.

"Not singing, I bet," said Kyle.

"Yes, singing," she said. "It's not the lead because this is my first show, but Mr. Palms says I have a few lines, and guess what?"

"What?" I asked.

"I'm going to sing a solo."

I couldn't believe it, and neither could the boys.

"They either don't hear well—" began Jon.

"Or no one else auditioned." Kyle laughed.

"Boys, stop teasing," Mom said. "What kind of a part is it, Allison?"

"Well, sort of a hillbilly girl, but on a farm. Oh, Mom, this is like a miracle, that I got in the play, I mean. I've got to practice every day, so I won't be able to help out much around the house for a while. Could B.J. take over my jobs?"

"Of course," Mom answered for me. "B.J. will be happy to."

I wouldn't be happy to at all. I didn't mind the extra work, but to think that we had to listen to that singing for a month longer was too much.

That night I secretly checked her horoscope. Under Allison's birth month, May, it read, "Relationship with family will be strained from April until May." That was for sure. "Oddly enough, though, your state of mind should be relatively cheerful. Part of this may be that you will become involved in some community activity" — of course, the play! — "and this will raise your status among neighbors and friends."

That settled it. There wasn't a thing I could do. Her astrological factors were favorable. It was written in the stars.

After about three weeks of rehearsing, Allison came home one evening and announced, "I've decided to use Love in the play."

"You can't bring a horse onstage," Kyle said.

"Why not?"

"Well, for one thing, she'll ruin the stage," he told her.

"Sure, with the horseshoes," explained Jon. "And speaking scientifically, that old stage would collapse with the weight."

"Besides, she's not housebroken," piped up Ethan.

"Now wait, everybody," Mom said. "Must it be a horse, Allison?"

"Well, it has to be a farm animal," she answered.

"Take Willie," said Ethan.

Allison was getting angry. "Not a dog, stupid. I said 'farm animal.' I have to have a *live* farm animal. Mr. Palms said it would add a lot to my big scene."

"That's a job for the prop department, Allison," Dad said. "It's not your responsibility. Let the prop people get you a farm animal."

But when Allison makes up her mind, she doesn't usually change it. Mom says she's persistent. Dad says she's stubborn. Her horoscope says that being under the sign of Taurus the bull, she's both. She's also spoiled.

Allison came home the following day and announced, "I've decided on a pig."

"A pig?" asked Jon.

"Yes. You're right. A horse is too big, but Mr. Palms said a pig would be perfect if I can get one."

"If *you* can get one?" asked Dad.

"Yes. Please, Dad, don't say no, and don't worry. I'll take care of everything."

When she said that, I knew what would happen. And it did. She was busy rehearsing, so Dad and I had to take care of everything. See what I mean about being spoiled? We were the ones who had to make the calls to find a piglet we could rent for the following weekend, when the musical was to be given. We finally located one at Mitchell's Farm, ten miles away.

Mom was nervous. "I don't think that child should carry a live piglet onstage without practice," she told Dad.

"Well, I can't afford to rent one for more than two days," Dad replied. "Do you know how much Mitchell is charging me? Per day? If you think I'm going to spend more than fifteen dollars on Mr. Palms' prop department, you're crazy."

Dad was getting nervous, too, I could tell.

But I had to agree with Dad. Then, I had to agree with Mom. I didn't envy Allison, trying to remember her lines while carrying a wiggly piglet, and then going into a song and dance.

The day of the dress rehearsal, Allison was absolutely impossible.

"It's a complete sellout," she bragged, "and we're going to be reviewed by the newspapers. I'll be a star, a star! And you know what Mr. Palms said, B.J.?"

I shook my head.

"He said, 'Break a leg, everybody.' "

"What?"

"That means good luck in show business."

"Well, your horoscope doesn't say anything about a broken leg," I assured her.

"What does it say, B.J.? Does it say I'll be a star?"

I opened my horoscope book. "It says, 'Things are apt to happen unless you watch your step. Be sensible. Keep your feet on the ground.' "

"Are you certain it doesn't say anything about me being a star?"

"Not a thing," I told her. I didn't finish the rest because then she really would have been unbearable. Besides, I honestly thought they'd made a mistake. It read, "Since Taurus rules the throat, singing is another common form of artistic expression and many famous singers were born under this sign."

Dad came home from the office early so he could drive over to Mitchell's Farm for the piglet. Mom insisted Allison stay home and rest. I went with Dad.

"Oh, I bet it's going to be so cute. Hurry, Dad. I want to take it to dress rehearsal tonight." Allison walked out to the car with us. "I'm going to get a little teeny basket, so I can carry it: I know, my Easter basket in the attic!" She dashed back into the house.

Dad and I drove to Mitchell's. Dad had phoned so he expected us, but he didn't expect so much trouble catching the thing. It was wild! And you should have seen Dad's face, and mine too, I guess, when we saw how big it was. That was no piglet. That was a full-grown pig!

"Dad," I whispered, "that's too big. What are we going to do?"

"Say, Mr. Mitchell," Dad said, "could you find a smaller pig?"

"Nope," he said, "she's the only one left. Been a good year. Sold 'em all but this one— the runt of the litter."

"Well, it's sure a big runt," said Dad.

Mitchell laughed. I didn't. How was Allison

going to carry that huge thing onstage? We put the pig in a crate in the back of the station wagon. *Phew!* What a smell. And it squealed all the way home. Easter basket? Allison would be lucky if she could get it in the laundry basket.

She was waiting for us. I saw her watching at the window. As soon as we drove in, she ran out, waving the Easter basket and cooing, "Let me see it, let me see my little baby."

She nearly fell over when she saw how big her little baby was. "Oh," she said. "I thought it was going to be a baby."

"It's the runt of the litter," sighed Dad and lifted the crate out of the car.

"But it won't fit in my basket," she wailed.

"Carry it under your arm," I said.

"I can't do that. It's too heavy." Allison looked as though she was going to cry.

By this time, Mom and the boys and Willie were inspecting the pig.

"Gosh, he's pretty big, Al." Jon was amazed.

"Well, what did you expect?" asked Ethan. "Pigs weigh two and a half pounds at birth and start doubling that first week. At five months, they weigh over two hundred pounds, and then—"

"That's enough, Ethan." Mom grabbed Willie as he tried to jump into the crate. "We'll think of something, don't you worry, Allison."

"Hey, I've got it!" said Kyle. "I've got it! We'll use Willie's collar and leash for the pig."

"Are you sure it will work?" Allison asked.

"Of course. It's an animal, isn't it?" said Ethan. "A pig is like any other animal. You put it on a leash and it's certainly going to follow you, isn't it? Just be sure to hang on."

The boys put Willie's collar on the pig. Allison got the leash. Dad put the crate back in the station wagon and drove Allison to the dress rehearsal.

Two hours later, he picked her up.

"How did it go, Allison?" Mom asked.

Allison was calm and collected. "Perfect. I was perfect. The pig was perfect. It followed me beautifully with the leash. Wherever I went, it went. Everything went perfectly — except for the lights. They couldn't get the stage lights working, but they'll be O.K. for tomorrow."

We all helped put the pig in the cellar. Nobody slept much. That pig grunted and squealed all night, and I kept hearing Allison go downstairs to the cellar. I guess she was trying to get to know the pig better.

"I've locked Willie in the laundry room," Mom said next morning. "I don't want him to make the pig nervous."

Make the *pig* nervous? Mom was beginning to sound like Allison. It was the pig that was making *everybody* nervous — including Willie.

"How's the star?" Dad asked as he came downstairs for breakfast.

"Fine," Mom answered. "She took the pig out for a little exercise."

"Morning, Mom. No clean stockings upstairs." Jon opened the laundry door.

Willie darted out, past us all, pushed open the screen door and started sniffing down the driveway.

Dad raced after him. "Watch that pig," he shouted to Allison. "I've got money invested in that thing."

We rescued Willie just in time.

The school bus honked. We had to catch it, and Dad had to get to his office. Poor Mom, she had to get the pig back in the cellar.

I guess she never did because when we got home, the pig was snoozing happily in Willie's old chair that Mom had pushed into the laundry room. Willie was hiding somewhere down in the cellar.

That night, opening night, Dad took Allison and the pig to the school first, then came back for us.

"Allison was right," he said. "The play is completely sold out. Why, the parking lot is crowded already. We'd better hurry."

Dad, Mom, the boys, and I found good seats near the side aisle, close to the stage. The music teacher, Stratton Swane, marched out with the Middle School Orchestra and everyone clapped. The auditorium lights dimmed, the stage lights went up, and then the music began.

"They fixed the lights, I see," whispered Dad.

The curtain went up, and we kept waiting and waiting for Allison. I could hear strange noises coming from backstage. It was that pig. I bet it was loose. I poked Ethan. "Where's Allison? Isn't she ever coming out?" The suspense was terrible.

Mom nudged me from the other side and pointed. Sure enough, there she came. Gee, I must admit, she looked great. She must have put on lots of makeup. And her eyes looked as big as saucers. She stepped forward and began singing. With the orchestra so loud, she didn't sound bad at all. And there was the pig, marching out from behind the side curtain. Instead of holding the leash in her hand, Allison had tied it around her waist, so she could use her arms and hands more freely when she sang.

The pig looked adorable. Allison was right.

It certainly added a lot to the scene. The audience loved it.

As soon as the pig got on the stage, though, it started this squirming and looked frightened. It tried to go back offstage, but Allison kept it right next to her. Then, right in the middle of her song, the pig started pulling Allison slowly off the stage. Just when she was doing so well, too. But Allison pulled that pig right back on and kept singing. Then the pig got really mad and started grunting and pulling Allison all over the place. The audience began laughing so loud I could barely hear Allison singing.

"What's the matter with that pig?" I asked Ethan.

"The lights," he said. "Pigs can't see well anyway, they have such small eyes. The stage lights are so bright they've completely blinded it. The pig doesn't know where it's going."

Ethan was right. I got so embarrassed I wanted to crawl under the seat. Instead, I tried covering my eyes, but I had to peek because I didn't want to miss anything.

Allison and the pig, by this time, were having a tug of war. She wouldn't stop singing and he wouldn't stop squealing, and they were going back and forth, all over the stage. Then the pig wrapped Allison around a prop tree. It fell over and almost landed on Stratton

Swane's head in the orchestra pit. The audience was howling and clapping louder than ever. Allison kept smiling and singing louder and trying to keep the pig and herself onstage.

But the pig kept trying to get back behind the curtain, away from the lights. Allison kept pulling the pig, and the pig kept pulling Allison. She'd let out one note onstage. The next would come from offstage. The audience was hysterical. Then, as Allison finally finished, the pig gave one tremendous pull and yanked my sister right off the stage—and off the floor. All you could see were two legs flying off somewhere backstage.

"I told her to keep her feet on the ground," I whispered to Ethan.

The audience went crazy. They applauded like mad.

"Encore, encore," everyone was shouting. I didn't think I could stand any more.

The next morning, Dad and I packed the pig in the crate to take it back to the farm.

"Don't you think we should keep it for a few days, Dad?" suggested Allison.

"Why, for heaven's sake?"

"Well, you never know, there might be a command performance for another show."

"Don't worry, Allison," I told her. "There's

not a thing in your horoscope that even hints at the possibility."

"Yeah, Allison and that pig were the biggest hams that stage will ever see." Kyle wise-cracked.

"Just a minute, you two," Mom spoke up. "Allison did have some kind of spark out there on that stage. We all have to agree to that."

Allison beamed. "Maybe I should take singing lessons, Mom, and go on the stage and become a star."

"Never," chuckled Dad.

"Why not, Dad?" wailed Allison.

"You'd never be a hit without the pig," he said. And we drove off to Mitchell's Farm.

The Gemini Child

"This child has an inquiring mind; he is continually asking questions with the intent of discovering the reason why." I turned the page of my *Family Horoscope Book* and continued reading. "These children have the ability to be clever, and often turn out to be progressive ... with an inventive genius." That was Jon all right! The genius of the family! Someday he'll be a famous scientist, or an astronaut, or maybe even a chiropractor. He's always doing interesting things—like when he nearly blew up the cellar with his chemistry set. Once he practically broke his leg when he jumped off the porch testing a parachute he'd made out of three umbrellas and a plastic tarpaulin.

Mom and Dad were relieved when he joined the science club at school and got interested in model rockets. At least it kept him out of trouble until school got out. Then he got this brilliant idea to send away for equipment to some big engineering company way out in Arizona and make rockets of his own.

I'd sent away for a new book on how to read tea leaves, so when I checked the mailbox every day, I'd carry Jon's packages up to him. You wouldn't believe how many arrived! His room was a mess. He had everything spread out all over the place. Jon would let me sit on his bed and watch him open the packages while he figured out where all the pieces went. So I promised him that he'd be the first one to have his tea leaves read.

By the middle of July, he'd spent most of his lawn-mowing money on bigger and bigger rockets from Arizona. He decided to go bankrupt and send for the biggest kit they had—the Super Streak.

"I'm going to have a real countdown with this one, B.J. After I finish putting it together, I'll order some gunpowder, build a launching pad, and set it up in the field."

"You mean, it will really take off?"

"That's what the catalog said."

"Then I'll invite the whole neighborhood to watch."

"Aw, I wouldn't do that, B.J.," Jon protested, but not very hard. I couldn't wait for Tony Spano to realize there was more to life than playing baseball — being an important scientist, like Jon, for instance. So I secretly planned to invite everybody I knew.

As soon as the Super Streak arrived, Jon began. He worked for days up in his room, and I watched him. He carved, he glued, he was brilliant.

"Wanna stick some decals on my rocket?" he asked when he finished the launching pad.

"Do I?" I ran and found a skull and crossbones I had stuck away in my bureau drawer. Jon didn't like it and made me use the American flag instead.

The day the postman brought the big red parcels of gunpowder for Jon's rocket, he brought a book for me, *Telling Fortunes in a Teacup*. I told Jon that meant something.

"Maybe your rocket will zoom to the moon, Jon."

"Don't be silly, B.J. But it should reach the woods in the state park over beyond our lower field."

Jon proudly pointed to the lettering on the box, "For Mature Persons Only." Then he carefully unwrapped the cardboard cylinders filled with gunpowder. He twisted some wires and stuck them into one end of the cylinder. Next he started clamping a lot of wires together. I was getting a little nervous even though Jon explained that it couldn't go off without a battery and the power switch. I kept thinking about his explosion in the cellar with the chemicals.

"When you finish, I'll read your tea leaves, Jon." I grabbed my book and ran down to the kitchen.

I put on the teakettle, tore open a tea bag, and put the dry leaves into a cup. Just as I was pouring the boiling water into the cup, Jon came downstairs. I handed him the cup of tea.

"Ugh, this tastes terrible," Jon sputtered.

"Drink it anyway," I said. "Only don't swallow the tea leaves. Now turn the teacup upside down, place it on the saucer, and turn it three times. O.K., give me the cup."

The book said the particles that remained inside the cup would make figures I could interpret into symbols. "The tea leaf reader needs imagination," it said. I was hoping I'd see a rocket, but I couldn't even find a tree or a flower. Finally I spotted something that looked like a fish. Thank goodness, a fish was one of the symbols listed in the book.

"It's a fish," I told Jon and pointed at a wiggly tea leaf. Then I read from my book.

"'*Fish:* This symbol predicts that some important event which will be very lucky to the consultant is going to take place.'"

"Why, that's my rocket launching," exclaimed Jon.

"You'll be famous," I told him and continued reading. "It says, 'Money should be involved, which will help overcome financial difficulties.'"

"Great!" said Jon. "I could use some money."

"But," I read on, "it also says that caution and diligence must be exercised."

"Naturally," Jon replied.

It had been hot and clear for days, not a speck of wind, perfect weather for a rocket launching. The next morning, Jon lugged all the rocket stuff down to the lower field. We planned the launching at noon when Dad would be home from his office for lunch. (He always comes home for lunch. Mom gave him peanut butter sandwiches for a whole week once, but he still comes home for lunch.) Nancy Tyler came over to help me call up the kids in the neighborhood. Then we spent the rest of the morning making brownies and lemonade to sell at the launching.

You should have seen the mob in the lower field by noon. Besides Tony Spano and his gang, Kyle and Ethan were there with all their friends. Allison had even invited her horse friend, Amy Walker. When Dad and Mom came down to join us, Jon began his speech.

"Welcome," he started.

I had to bite my lip to keep from giggling. When I get nervous, I always giggle.

"Welcome to the first rocket launching on Viewland Drive. Watch for the following stages: First, the thrust, when the rocket takes off. The second stage as the rocket coasts upward. The third and final stage, as the red and white parachute is released. Thank you all for coming. And now, let's blast off!"

Everyone laughed. Nancy and I clapped.

The rocket looked wonderful. If you squinted, it looked like a real one, pointing up to the sky, held by a guiding tube and a heavy wire that jutted out from Jon's launching pad.

Jon was kneeling on the ground, checking the angle of the rocket and the wires. Holding the switch in one hand, he started the countdown.

"Ten! Nine!"

Nancy and I started counting with him.

"Eight! Seven!"

Mom and Dad joined in.

"Six! Five!"

The whole neighborhood was chanting. It was so loud we could hear an echo coming back from the park woods.

"Four! Three! Two! One! Blast off!"

But it didn't.

Jon frantically adjusted the wires, the tube, the battery. Nothing helped.

We all tried to be polite and waited, hoping something would make the thing go off.

That smark aleck, Tony Spano, from down the road, stood up and said, "Welcome to the first rocket-launching cancellation on Viewland Drive."

Everybody thought that was pretty funny — everybody but Jon and me.

"Better luck next time, Jon!" Tony Spano walked off, taking his baseball team with him.

Dad went back to his office. Nancy went home. I was so upset I forgot to sell the lemonade and brownies.

After they had all gone, I told Jon I was going to send *Telling Fortunes in a Teacup* right back.

"Oh, I'm not discouraged, B.J. I've just got to find out what's wrong."

So, every day for two weeks, Jon and I went down to the field with the rocket. But it never worked. I gave up. But Jon didn't.

*　　　*　　　*

At the beginning of August—boy, was it hot —Mom was in the kitchen baking, and I was on the phone with Nancy Tyler, when I heard Jon shouting.

"Hey! Hey, everybody! Hey!" he was yelling.

I dropped the receiver. Mom and I rushed to the back door.

"It blasted off?" I shouted.

Jon nodded. I was so happy I started jumping up and down.

Mom gave Jon a hug. "Too bad no one was there to see it, Jon."

"You wouldn't believe how high it went. And what an explosion! Guess I didn't push the wire in far enough before. But this morning I got so mad, I just took that wire and—" Jon was babbling on.

I began hopping around and singing, "For he's a jolly good fellow." I would have stood on my head, if I could.

"Where did it come down?" Mom asked.

"Way over in the woods someplace," Jon said. "Come on, B.J., let's get it."

"I left Nancy Tyler hanging."

"Go help Jon," Mom said. "I'll tell her all about it."

We ran through the field, into the back part of the park woods. After about an hour, I spotted the red and white parachute.

"There it is, Jon." I pointed up to a small branch on top of a huge pine tree.

"Great! No problem. I'll get it." Jon climbed up.

"Catch, B.J."

Down, down, floated Jon's first flying rocket and landed at my feet.

"It's in fine shape, Jon!" I yelled up to him.

"Boy, you should see the view up here. It's fantastic." Jon called down. "There's our barn and the house... Hey, B.J., you should see all the smoke rising. Hey, there's a fire!"

"Is it our house, Jon? Is our house on fire?" I'm scared silly of fires.

"No, it's not our house, but it does look like our field. It sure is our whole field." Jon scrambled down.

We ran like anything back through the woods, up the dirt road toward our house. We heard fire sirens getting louder and louder as we got closer. I never saw so much smoke. And there, ahead of us, was our whole field and fire everywhere. The dry grass was crackling like crazy.

"I hope it doesn't get any closer to the barn," I screamed. "Love's in there."

By the time we made it to the field, the fire engines had come, followed by the whole neighborhood. Mom had a bucket of water in one hand and was swatting at the burning grass with a wet towel with the other. Kyle and Ethan were slapping at it with brooms and the neighbors were stamping on flames at the edge. Then the firemen hooked up the hose to the hydrant on the main road and squirted everything. In no time at all, it was over.

It's a good thing Allison was at Amy Walker's house. She would have pitched a fit if she had seen how close the fire had crept to the barn.

"Who's been burning brush this time of year?" I heard Larry June, the fire chief, ask Mom. "I'll have to turn in my report."

"I can't imagine how it started, Larry," Mom apologized. "Would you and the men like some fresh tollhouse cookies?"

"Nope, gotta get back to the fire station. But if I was you, I'd check on how this fire started. Came mighty close to burning the barn."

Mom nodded. By then, half the crowd was gone. She sighed, picked up her bucket, and said, "B.J., tell the boys there will be a family conference tonight after dinner. Your father and Allison will be home by then."

I knew by the way she looked and spoke that this was going to be the most serious family conference yet.

After dinner that night, we all sat around in the keeping room. That's an old-fashioned name for a family room, and our house is so old, that's what Mom and Dad decided to call it. Mom spoke first.

"As you've probably guessed, this conference is called because of the fire this afternoon. Not only did it endanger the life of the horse in the barn, but we caused a great deal of trouble for the fire department. If that hay had caught on fire, the whole barn would have gone up, just like that." Mom snapped her fingers. I'd never seen her so upset and angry.

"If," she continued, "there is someone in this room responsible for that fire, I want him to admit it."

There was an awful silence. I looked at Kyle. Why, he was getting as red as a beet. And Ethan sure looked funny. I bet they were smoking! Mom looked as though she thought they were too. I closed my eyes to see if I could get a vision or something.

"We'll sit here until someone confesses." Dad sounded like we were all in court.

The suspense was terrible.

"I bet you think it's me," Kyle blurted out,

"smoking. But honest, Mom, I wasn't. I wasn't even near the field. Ask Eeth."

Ethan turned red too. "Well, we were near the field, Kyle. But we didn't have any matches, Mom. We were playing catch with Tony Spano."

"Don't look at me," said Allison. "I wasn't even home."

"And B.J. and I were in the park looking for the rocket. In fact, I was up in the tree when I saw smoke. Right, B.J.?"

"Right, Jon," I answered. "We weren't anywhere near the field."

There was silence again.

"Wait a minute!" Jon jumped up. "*I* started the fire. It wasn't Kyle or Ethan, it was me."

"You, Jon?" asked Dad.

"Sure. I left the battery switch on."

"What battery switch?"

"The one I used to fire my rocket."

"A battery couldn't start a fire."

"No, but the wire clamped to the battery could," explained Jon. "It gets as red hot as a toaster wire. I forgot to turn it off."

We were all so relieved that it was Jon, and not Kyle or Ethan, that we burst out singing, "For he's a jolly good fellow." I still don't know who we were singing to.

Mom apologized to Kyle and Ethan for suspecting them. But then she had to give a half-hour lecture on how careless Jon was. She told him if he was going to be a scientist he'd have to be more careful with explosives and things. It was worth it though, 'cause after the lecture we got the tollhouse cookies, plus vanilla ice cream, to celebrate the blastoff. I noticed the boys got the biggest helpings. But nobody complained, not even Allison.

A few days later, Dad received a letter from the fire department.

Dear Sir,
    We are enclosing two tickets for our annual Firemen's Ball. We know you will want to support this fine organization with an appropriate contribution.

                Yours sincerely,
                Larry June, Fire Chief

"Don't worry, Dad, I'll pay for the tickets with my allowance," offered Jon.

"I bet they'll send them every year from now on," said Ethan.

I was about to say, "I told you so," and make Jon admit my tea leaf reading had been amazingly accurate. The important event wasn't that lucky, but my prediction that "money would be involved" had come true. Wasn't Jon's money going to help overcome the financial difficulties of the fire department? And really, if Jon had been more cautious and diligent, like the tea leaves said, the fire never would have started in the first place. I decided not to say anything.

Jon appreciated that. He said I could read his tea leaves again, but I didn't bother. I practiced once or twice on Nancy, but she kept choking on them. Besides, it was almost time to go back to school. I didn't mention it to Nancy—she'd be terribly disappointed—but I was getting a little bored with being gifted.

Willie, the Lion-Hearted

Once school started, I didn't have much time to study and improve my magical talents, but I always managed to check my horoscope. This time it said, "It will be a great day for relaxing, although the morning hours might get a little hectic." It was accurate as usual. It was a pretty hectic morning all right.

When we got home from church, the telephone was ringing. It stopped just as we pushed open the back door. It must have been ringing for some time, because the caned seat of Mom's rocker was chewed up, and Willie was up on the sofa digging into the cushions.

Allison started to vacuum up the mess, but Willie ran after her, snapping at the vacuum. When Dad tried to wallop him with the newspaper, Willie grabbed it and ran out to the kitchen. There, he began spinning around, biting his tail, because he couldn't reach the electric can opener Mom was using.

Dad was furious. "That dog has got to be trained. I've a good mind to have all his teeth pulled out."

Nobody paid any attention because Dad's been saying that for years. I had to agree with him, though. That Willie was getting out of hand.

Things calmed down after dinner. We were all in the keeping room relaxing.

"Listen to this, Jack. 'What a wonderful feeling to have your dog come when you give the command.' "

"Hmm? What's that, Dorothy?"

"It's an advertisement for Dog Obedience School." Mom read on, " '...to teach your dog to be a better member of the human family.' "

"That's Willie's trouble," mumbled Dad. "He already thinks he's a member of the human family."

"It's too late, Mom," piped up Kyle. "Willie's old."

"It's never too late." Mom tore the ad out of the paper.

"When was Willie born?" I asked her.

"I can't remember the year, but it was in July, I think."

"Then he's a Leo — Leo the Lion." I flipped back the pages of my horoscope book to July.

"Willie, your sign is associated with the lion, king of the jungle, and it is as a king you see yourself."

Jon was lying on the rug next to me, doing his homework. "You can't read the horoscope of a dog, stupid."

I ignored him and read on, " 'Born under the sign that rules show people, you see yourself as the star of life's show. Above all, you are very sensitive and want to be noticed.' "

"That's it," said Allison. "He needs an audience. That's why he bites things and misbehaves." She grabbed Willie and tried to snuggle him but he snarled at her and crawled under the cobbler's bench. "Don't worry, Willie. I love you and understand. I'll knit you something so you'll know I love you. Willie needs attention."

"You both need an analyst," moaned Kyle and turned on the television.

"It's his ears."

"What's that, Ethan?" Dad asked.

"A dog can hear sounds two hundred and fifty yards away that people can't hear beyond twenty-five yards."

"Sure," Jon said. "It's right here in my science book. 'Dogs can hear sounds that vibrate at frequencies many more times a second than humans.' "

"Which means?" asked Mom.

"It's his ears," repeated Ethan. "There's something wrong with them."

"Nonsense," said Mom. "B.J., how would you like to take Willie to Dog Obedience School?"

"Who, me? Never."

"I'd pay for those new books you've been wanting to send away for."

That did it. I really needed some new books; especially the one Nancy had been talking about — *Destiny and Dreams*.

Mom made arrangements in the morning and on Tuesday evening dropped Willie and me off at the Middle School Gym. It looked different at night with all the lights on, but it smelled the same.

Some ladies in baggy pants and sneakers were rolling out narrow rubber carpets and trying to make a circle with them. On their red sweatshirts was printed in big white letters, *Happy Kennels Dog Obedience School*.

One was standing behind a small table on the other side of the gym. She beckoned to me.

Willie was a nervous wreck. He'd never seen so many people or heard so much yelping. I carried him across the gym. The lady was selling the special leashes and choke collars you had to use in class. As I put Willie down to pay for them, a whistle blew. "Mrs. Popper wants to begin." The assistant nodded toward the largest lady in baggy pants, standing in the center of the circle.

I bent down to put on Willie's new collar. He was gone. I quickly checked under the table. No Willie. I glanced around the crowded gym. Where was that dog? I called softly, "Willie, Willie." I got a little louder when I realized Mrs. Popper and the dogs and everybody were standing in place, waiting for me.

Mrs. Popper impatiently pointed to the tumbling mat hanging on the wall under the basketball backboard. I ran over and pulled Willie out from behind the mat.

"This training will be especially good for a dog like that," she announced to the class as I carried Willie to the circle. "He has been too protected. He needs to be more aggressive. When this course is over, that dog will feel like a king." Mrs. Popper sounded like she had been reading my horoscope book. "What's his name?"

"Leo—I mean, Willie."

"Willie?"

I nodded.

"Willie will be a performer, a regular trouper. He will be obedient and come when he is called."

Everybody looked at us and smiled. I smiled back and hoped I didn't look as much like Willie as they all looked like their dogs.

"Tonight we're going to teach our dogs to heel. Say the name of your dog, then say heel, then step forward. If the dog doesn't come, jerk the leash. Ready? Tell your dog to heel."

"Willie, heel." I stepped forward. Willie didn't budge. I jerked the leash. Willie sat there. I walked back to try to reason with him.

Mrs. Popper ran over to me shouting, "Are you going to train the dog, or is the dog going to train you? Heel your dog."

I had a funny feeling Mrs. Popper didn't like Willie. She was probably a Pisces. Pisces don't get along with Leos.

"Willie, heel," I commanded and started forward. I jerked the leash so hard it unsnapped. Willie made a dash for the door, practically knocking over Mrs. Popper. The cocker spaniel in front of me and the wire-haired terrier behind me took off too. There was a lot of screaming and heeling and barking.

"Linda, come," the woman next to me was shouting.

"Simmy, come," commanded the wire-haired terrier's master.

"Willie, come," I yelled.

Linda and Simmy came trotting back but

Willie kept going, straight out the gym door.

I found him hiding under a parked car. We got back to the circle just as Mrs. Popper was saying, "That's all for tonight. Communicate with your dogs. It's fun, fun. Let your dog know it's fun." Then she spotted us. "But we must be in control. Remember, a happy dog is a trained dog. Just watch your dog's reactions. I've never seen a tail go down in this class. Good night, all." Mrs. Popper laughed gaily and Willie's tail slowly dropped between his legs.

The next week I sneaked Willie in between a German shepherd and a Dalmatian so Mrs. Popper wouldn't notice us. She had just started speaking.

"All training begins from the sitting position. If you can't get your dog under this control, you can't teach him anything."

Then Mrs. Popper gave the command to sit. Willie turned over on his back, put his four legs up in the air, and waited to be scratched. I saw Mrs. Popper coming at us again, so I quickly turned him up and tried to get him to sit by pushing down on his back.

"No, no," screamed Mrs. Popper, rushing at me. "Never try to get a dog to sit that way. Take his back legs like this and push them under—"

I tried to say I wouldn't do that if I were you when Willie growled and tried to take a nip out of Mrs. Popper's arm.

"Bad dog, bad dog, Willie." Mrs. Popper backed away.

"He's very sensitive when you touch his hind legs," I told her.

"Did you hear that, class?" she asked. "Never let any part of your dog be sensitive. Remember, you have to show the dog you are in control." Mrs. Popper walked back to the middle of the ring, rubbing her elbow, and calling, "Pierre, Pierre."

A little black poodle lying on a jacket in the corner jumped up and trotted over to her.

"Pierre, heel." Pierre heeled.

"Pierre, forward." Pierre went forward.

"Halt, sit, heel, down, stay. Good dog, good dog, Pierre." Mrs. Popper lifted her toy poodle up in the air. The class applauded. Willie growled again and looked the other way.

"Our time is up," she announced. "I want you to practice every day with your dog. When you've completed this course, your dog will perform like Pierre and receive his diploma."

"Diploma?" I asked the lady next to me who looked like a German shepherd.

"Yes, isn't it exciting? There's a graduation in four weeks and all the dogs get a diploma."

"Graduation?"

"That's right. A judge will be here to score the dogs."

"Score the dogs?"

"Of course. You get so many points for each exercise, you know, like heeling or sitting. My, everyone's left but us. Good night." She turned to her dog. "Tulip, heel." Off she went with Tulip heeling at her side.

I picked up Willie. He was so tired I didn't think he'd make it out the gym. Mom was waiting for us.

"Never again," I said as I slammed the car door.

Mom was smart enough not to say anything.

The following Tuesday, Mrs. Popper explained to the class, "When the judge comes for graduation, one of the exercises you will have to do is the figure eight. This is important because it teaches your dog to walk at ease in and out of crowds. Now first, we're going to take turns winding in and out around each dog and owner, straight down the row."

All the other dogs performed beautifully. We were the last.

"Willie, heel." I stepped forward, gave a big yank on the leash, and started down the line. I didn't dare look back at Willie. I just kept pulling and praying. I guess that's why I didn't realize he'd been sliding on the slippery gym floor upside down, all the way.

The class laughed, but Mrs. Popper didn't think it was so funny. "Everyone, circle to the right," she ordered. "Now circle to the left. Now the right, now the left." Willie was getting so confused and upset that he started spinning around in circles and biting his tail, just like he does when the can opener works. Mrs. Popper finally had to heel him into the corner for the rest of the evening.

The next day, when I came home from school, Mom was sitting at the kitchen desk staring at the phone.

"What's the matter, Mom? You look funny."

"I'm disappointed, that's all. Mrs. Popper called to say Willie won't possibly have enough points to graduate and that you shouldn't take him to any more of the classes. They'd be too advanced for him." Mom put on the teakettle and looked down at Willie. "Don't worry, Willie, we can enroll you again. Then you'll graduate and get your diploma."

"Don't count on me, Mom."

"No, I'll do it myself. I'll write Mrs. Popper tonight and enroll Willie for the next session." And she did.

Friday night after supper, somebody buzzed the door bell. Willie woke up and followed me, barking and biting anything he could dig his teeth into.

It was special delivery. I signed the yellow slip and ran back to the keeping room.

"It's for Willie," I told everybody, and pulled a white paper out of the large envelope. "Hey, it's a diploma from the Happy Kennels Dog Obedience School, and a note from Mrs. Popper. She says, on second thought, she felt Willie should have his diploma. And Mom, she's returning your application fee because there's no more room in her next class."

"That dog certainly doesn't deserve a diploma," said Dad as Willie jumped up and tried to grab the paper.

"Willie, sit," I ordered. Willie sat!

"Willie, heel." I started forward and Willie followed, wagging his tail.

"Down," I shouted and Willie went down.

"Yea, Willie," said Kyle.

"Good dog, good dog, Willie," said Jon, laughing.

"And I've got a surprise for you," Allison said. "Here, Willie, I've knitted you some earmuffs." She put them on him. He sure looked ridiculous.

The phone rang. We all waited for Willie to start biting things, but he just lay there. It rang again.

It was Nancy Tyler. "It's a miracle," I told her. "I'll have to call you back."

"See," I told them all, "he is trained."

"It's his ears," said Ethan. "Allison put earmuffs on him and that's why he's trained."

"Well, maybe," admitted Mom, "but he still deserves his diploma and I'm going to frame it for you, Willie."

Willie turned over on his back, put his legs up in the air, and waited to be scratched.

The next night I spotted a full-page ad in the evening paper saying that the Happy Kennels Dog Obedience School had openings for their next fall class. What I had suspected all along was true. Mrs. Popper really was a Pisces, and she just couldn't take another class with Willie!

I was about to tell Mom. Then I decided not to say anything. Not in front of Willie, anyway. You see, he's a Leo, and Leos are very sensitive.

Black Clouds
on a Crystal Ball

I had to be honest. I never did see anything in that crystal ball. I'd only pretend I saw a ship when I told Kyle he was going on a long voyage. The cruise tickets were a coincidence.

I had wasted Aunt Maud's five dollars—and the old horse's bit I'd given Allison for her birthday wasn't worth half of what I'd borrowed from her for the books. It cost fifty cents at a tag sale.

I took the crystal ball out of the secret hiding place and decided to give it one more chance to work. It rested against the dark velvet cloth on my bedstand. The light from the window fell over my shoulder onto the crystal, just like the book said it should.

I was about to begin concentrating when the activity school bus stopped out front. I peeked out the window.

There are times when I can't stand my sister, like right then. She was running up the driveway waving her arms over her head, like a scarecrow, only fatter. I could tell something had happened. She had that crazy look in her eyes and she was talking to herself.

"Mom, Mom?" she yelled and slammed the door.

"She's shopping," I shouted down at her.

"Oh. B.J., guess what?"

"What?" I got up to close my bedroom door so she wouldn't come in.

"No, don't guess what," she said.

I heard her opening the refrigerator. "It's too important. I'll wait and make an announcement when the whole family's home."

I began my gazing. The crystal ball seemed to be getting cloudy. The clouds turned black! I checked my book, *Secrets of the Crystal Ball*. Black clouds were a certain omen of coming unpleasant events. They warn of impending danger, loss, trouble, and grief. I got goose bumps. Then I had a premonition. The clouds had something to do with Allison's news!

After dinner, she made her announcement. "There's going to be a horse show at the Grange Fair next week. I'm going to enter Love."

81

"That's nothing," said Ethan. "I'm entering my pumpkins and squash."

"Not as an exhibit, silly. I'm going to ride Love in the show."

"But you don't know enough about showing," Dad said.

"I know everything," she boasted. "I'll just need to buy a hard hat, a riding outfit, some boots, oh, and I may have to hire a trailer to haul Love over to the fairgrounds. But don't worry, Amy will share the expense."

"Amy Walker?" Mom asked.

"Uh-huh. We've been practicing for weeks, so Amy thinks we should enter lots of classes. We'll probably win all the ribbons."

"That horse of yours is too fat to show," said Jon.

"You're both too fat," Ethan told her.

I agreed with Ethan. Being a Taurus, Allison has strong inclinations to overeat.

Allison pulled in her stomach. "I'll go on a diet," she told us.

And she did. By the end of the week she had lost five pounds and talked Dad into paying for her share of the trailer. With the money she earned helping around the house, she bought a complete riding outfit at the Salvation Army.

Two days before the fair, we found out that Lida Pratt was entering the show.

"But she's got a beautiful bay thoroughbred," I objected.

"So what?" asked Allison.

"Love is a backyard horse. It's not fair."

"Love is a beautiful white mare," Allison replied.

"Yeah, and she's got manure stains all over her from rolling in the field," said Ethan.

"Don't worry, I'll give her a bath."

"It won't come off," Jon said. "The chemicals in the manure that makes it valuable for fertilizer also have qualities that adhere to —"

"Never mind," interrupted Allison. "You'll see, it'll come off."

Allison hosed Love down in the driveway, but even with Mom's detergent, Love looked more yellow than white.

"Why don't you bleach her?" I asked.

"Are you crazy?" Allison shrieked. "It would burn her skin off. But," she paused, "I could put some bluing on her."

"Huh?"

"You know, like Tony Spano's grandmother uses. It makes white hair silver gray. I'll ask Mom to pick some up at the beauty parlor tomorrow."

"Well, you'd better do something fast," I told her. "You only have one day left."

When we came home from school Friday,

Mom handed Allison a bottle of bluing. "Antonio says to be certain to read the directions. I have to drive over to the Grange with the boys to enter Ethan's vegetables. B.J., you help Allison. Oh, and don't forget to turn on the stew at four forty-five."

We ran out to the barn. Allison took Love out of the stall and hitched her up to the crossties. "I'll put the bluing on. You can clean out the stall, B.J."

That made me mad. "I'm not doing all the mucking out. I quit." I decided to go over to the Spanos to see if Marianne's rabbits had babies again.

At four thirty I remembered the stew and dashed home. As I turned on the stove, Allison came in, sobbing.

"What's the matter?" I asked.

"I'm not going to be in the horse show."

"Why not?"

"She turned blue."

"Who?"

"Love."

"Blue?"

"Dark blue."

I raced out to the barn with her. She was right. Love was blue, dark blue. "Didn't you read the directions?" I asked, picking up the bottle. "It says, 'Use sparingly.' "

"I didn't have the light on," she wailed. "I thought it said 'daringly.' "

"Well, get some soap and wash it off."

"I did."

"You did? There must be a way to get it off. Call Antonio."

Allison was too upset, so I did.

"He says you must have forgotten to add the water," I told her. "But don't worry, there's three remedies, bleach, dye, or rinse."

"We can't bleach. I told you that before. A horse's skin is too sensitive."

"How about shaving it all off?" I asked.

Allison wailed louder.

"Well then, get a color rinse. You can always wash it out."

"What do you mean, 'color rinse'?"

"Antonio says it's a temporary hair coloring. It rinses in and shampoos out."

We were lucky. Eddie Dowling stopped by to see if Kyle was home. He said he'd be happy to drive us downtown.

There was a color chart on the drugstore counter and plenty of shades to choose from. I suggested Plush Brown or Dark Blaze, but Allison asked the clerk which shade they had the most of and charged six bottles of Hot Chestnut.

It was easy to squeeze the stuff out of the

plastic bottles and sponge it onto Love. It dried right away.

"Oh, B.J., it's wonderful. She's like a thoroughbred, a chestnut thoroughbred, and she's gorgeous," said Allison.

Mom, Dad, and the boys didn't think so. They were horrified. But after we told them what had happened, they admitted that a brown horse was better than a blue one.

That night, I got out my crystal ball and set it up on the black velvet. They were there again — those black clouds.

Saturday morning, Allison's alarm went off at six. I got up to help her braid Love's tail and mane. Then Dad took some pictures of Allison dressed in her riding outfit.

She looked all right considering the person who wore the jodhpurs before must have been a few sizes larger, and the previous owner of the jacket a few sizes smaller. I thought the hat sat a little high on her head, but the strap under her chin would hold it on — if it didn't choke her. Kyle said the boots looked like gunboats. I thought they were a bargain at seventy-five cents.

Allison posed again with Love as she walked her out the driveway to Mr. Potowski's trailer.

He'd already picked up Amy and Silver. Love boarded the trailer like a dream. They had trouble closing the door, though. Love didn't quite fit. Her tail hung out over the back. Allison tied a red ribbon on it and hopped up front with Amy and Mr. Potowski.

We followed right behind them in the station wagon, laughing at Love's tail flying out over the back. Suddenly, manure started flying, right at us.

"Close the windows," I yelled.

"Turn on the windshield wiper," shouted Ethan.

Nothing more could possibly happen, I thought. Then I remembered the dark clouds and knew it was only the beginning.

Allison and Amy entered all the classes, but didn't win all the ribbons. Amy finally got a third prize in the Walk-Trot class. Allison got a sixth. There were only seven in the class, but at least it was encouraging.

"Wait until the last class, the Outside Jumping Course with Obstacles," Allison said. "I'll win that for sure."

I hadn't noticed before how dark it had become. I'd been too busy keeping track of Allison. I kept looking for a white horse instead of a hot chestnut thoroughbred.

Suddenly it started to sprinkle; that's when I glanced up and saw the black clouds, like in my crystal ball.

The jumping class was announced. Mom was worried. The jumps didn't look a bit like the small ones Allison had been practicing with at home. The course wasn't that simple either. It began at the gate of the fairgrounds, but went outside, up, and around some hills and then back onto the grounds.

We watched as Lida, Amy, and the others, one by one took the course. Some knocked over the jumps and top rails. One horse refused to go over the stone wall and the rider landed in a hedge. I didn't blame Mom for being worried. Allison could never make the course, especially in all this rain.

Allison's number was called over the loudspeaker. She smiled and trotted over to the starting position. The judge signaled her on and she took off like a bolt. Up and over the fences she went, clearing them easily. By now, it was pouring. It didn't matter though, Love was performing like the thoroughbred she had become. Mom and Dad were clapping, and the boys were cheering Allison on. She disappeared for a while over a hill, but I knew by the applause of the crowd she had made another jump perfectly. She cantered back around the hill with one last and highest jump to make. I crossed my fingers and closed my eyes and knew that no crystal ball or black clouds could keep my sister from winning. The crowd cheered. She cleared it! We knew she had won the trophy even before they announced it over the loudspeaker.

Allison leaned forward in the saddle and hugged Love. She looked toward us and waved. I nearly collapsed. Half of her face had turned dark brown. As the judge handed her the silver cup and patted Love's neck, his hand turned brown too. It was the Hot Chestnut rinse. It was washing off.

Beaming, Allison trotted out of the ring, not noticing Lida Pratt talking to the judge and refusing second prize.

Then, over the loudspeaker, we heard, "Attention. Will Allison Pinkerton please return to the ring? There has been a default. According to Conduct Rule 3, Section 12, any change of color or markings other than mane, tail, or hoof is prohibited. Miss Pinkerton must forfeit her prize to Miss Pratt."

"What are they talking about?" asked Mom.

"It's the coloring. I guess we shouldn't have done it."

Mom turned to Dad. "You're a lawyer, can't you do something?"

"It's the rule, I can't change that," said Dad.

Allison explained to the judge and all the officials, but it didn't make any difference. When Mr. Potowski drove up with the trailer, she was still crying, and Love was bluer than ever.

Ethan won first prize for his pumpkins and first prize for his zucchini, so the day wasn't a total loss.

The next morning, when Allison and I went out to feed Love and give her a rubdown, she had a big blue ribbon hanging on each side of her halter.

"Now, wasn't that sweet of Ethan," Allison sighed.

"Yep," I said, "and they just match your horse."

I phoned Nancy to tell her about seeing the dark clouds on my crystal ball and everything that happened at the grange.

"That's great, B.J. I'm going to write a letter to one of those TV interviewers. I'll arrange an appearance for you."

"Really, Nancy?"

"I'll write the letter tonight. Keep practicing!" She hung up.

I tried and tried, but I couldn't get the black clouds to come back. I realized why. I wasn't using the black velvet cloth. It wasn't magic at all. It wasn't black clouds I had seen either. It was the reflection of the black cloth on the crystal ball!

The next day at school, I told Nancy the truth. It was all a hoax.

"It's O.K., B.J.," Nancy said. "I didn't write the letter yet anyway. But you mustn't be discouraged. You are gifted, you know. You can't throw away your talent. Here, I got this for you at the library." She shoved a book at me. "Anybody can gaze into a crystal ball, but not everybody can practice — witchcraft."

Meowner, the Black Cat;
or
Who Let the Cat in the House?

If I was truly gifted, and had E.S.P. like Nancy said, how come I wasn't warned about the notice in the mail Monday from Mr. Jakeman? Mom knew I was failing Language Arts before I did. And she was furious.

"There will be no more hocus-pocus in this house, young lady. And if I catch you reading any more of those fortune-telling books before your marks improve, I'll throw out every book on your shelf!" Mom meant business.

I took the book on witchcraft back to the library and exchanged it for *Little Women*.

The next day, when Mr. Jakeman offered extra credit if someone would make a sound tape to illustrate speech habits, I thought I'd better volunteer. All I had to do was borrow a cassette recorder from the Library Media Center and fill a tape with different voices.

When I got off the school bus and spotted Meowner sitting outside the back door, a wonderful idea came to me—an apparition, Nancy calls it. Why not be really creative and surprise Mr. Jakeman by starting the tape with animal sounds, and work up to humans?

I had to check to make certain Mom wasn't home. You see, Meowner's this straggly black cat Amy Walker had to get rid of. So she left it at our house. Mom had a fit. We have to keep the cat in the barn with the horse because Mom's allergic. Besides, cats upset Willie, and Mom says it's not fair to make him adjust at his age.

The station wagon wasn't in the driveway. Nobody was home. And Willie was sound asleep under the dining-room table. It was safe to bring the cat in. I put her down on the sofa and took the cassette out of my school bag.

"Now purr into this microphone, Meowner, come on, that's a good kitty. Say *meow, meow*."

The microphone must have tickled her whiskers because she started sneezing like anything.

I remembered reading about cats sneezing in *Omens of Yesteryear*. I ran upstairs to get it. Halfway back down I also remembered what Mom said about my fortune-telling books. I decided she wouldn't mind as long as I only used it as a reference.

"Listen to what it says about you, Meowner." I held her in my lap. " 'Black cats bring good fortune. If one crosses your path it denotes good luck, as does a cat that sneezes. But beware of the black cat that meows at midnight.' "

I closed the book and gave Meowner a hug. She began to purr. I pushed down the record button. "Just a few little meows," I whispered.

Willie wandered into the keeping room and jumped up on the sofa. Meowner jumped over him. He started chasing her all over the place. It was great. You never heard such sounds. I followed them into the kitchen, thinking how pleased Mr. Jakeman would be with the tape. Wouldn't you know! Mom came in the back door with the groceries, tripped over Meowner, and dropped the bag with the eggs. They smashed to the floor.

Meowner darted out the door, and Willie began licking up the eggs.

"Who let that cat in the house?" Mom sneezed and ran to the sink for a sponge.

"She crossed your path. But don't worry, that's good luck. And did you know cracked eggs can be used as a protective spell?"

Mom threw the egg shells in the garbage and didn't say a thing.

I could tell she wasn't in a very good mood, so I went back to the keeping room with the tape recorder. It was still running. Well, I could turn on the television and catch a few voices at least.

"Young lady, if you have nothing better to do, you can set the table."

"I'm doing my homework."

Mom walked in from the kitchen. "B.J. Pinkerton, how can you say that? You know you're watching an old Humphrey Bogart movie."

"It's part of my homework."

"I suppose this is, too?" Darn it, Mom picked up the book on omens I'd left on the sofa.

I decided it would be easier to set the table than explain.

After dinner, I taped Dad snoring in his reclining chair and Allison fighting with the boys. I couldn't believe Humphrey Bogart took up so much of my tape. I rewound it, put the cassette on the end table with my school things, and went up to bed.

Our house is so old and big we each get our

own bedroom. They're all small, though. Mine is the smallest, but I love it. It's at the end of the hall, near the back stairs. The back stairs lead to the kitchen. It makes it easy, when you're hungry, to sneak down and get something. I can tell when everyone has gone to bed because Mom turns on the dishwasher last thing. And I know every stage by heart.

First, there's a big clunk, then a couple of gurgles and water swooshes in. Then the swishing starts with the clinkety clunks until the rinse cycle.

I was so tired I fell asleep right after the first big clunk.

I woke up on the floor, all mixed up in my blankets. I'd had a horrible nightmare about cats. Thank goodness it was a short one. The dishwasher hadn't even gone through the entire wash cycle. I needed a piece of lemon pie to calm my nerves, so I tiptoed downstairs. I was finishing the last bite when I heard this meowing and scratching. It was that cat. The poor thing was freezing. Allison must have locked her out of the barn when she fed Love.

"Come on, Meowner." I could hear the old clock in the keeping room strike midnight. I don't know why, but I shivered. I turned off the light in the kitchen and carried the cat upstairs.

Meowner, lying on my bed, reminded me of my nightmare. I had to find out what dreaming about cats meant before I went back to sleep— no matter what Mom said about my books. I checked the dream chart in *Destiny and Dreams*. It was pretty bad. *"Cats:* Trust no one. Even your best friends will be disloyal. You will be disappointed, let down, and experience losses. You may begin to hear strange voices. If the cat is seen fighting, you will be robbed."

I put the book back on my bedstand and turned on the light. Meowner jumped off the bed and strolled down the hallway. I sure was glad to get rid of her. I pulled my blankets way up over my head.

I heard a strange noise. At first, I thought I must be dreaming again. I sat up. No, I was awake all right. And I was hearing voices, just like my dream book said I might. I hopped out of bed and ran down the hall so I could tell everybody. Before I had a chance to turn on the hall light, I heard the voices again. Trouble was, they were coming from downstairs. I leaned over the banister. Of course! I should have known. It was burglars! We were being robbed, like my dream book predicted. Hadn't Willie and the cat been fighting? And that was the bad luck Meowner was meowing about when the clock was striking midnight! No wonder I got goose bumps.

I dashed across the hall into Mom and Dad's bedroom.

"Mom, Mom," I whispered. "I heard voices. I thought it was my E.S.P., but a black cat was meowing at midnight and there's burglars in the house."

"What?"

"Somebody's downstairs."

"Jack, wake up." Mom shook Dad.

"Shh, I'm sleeping," grumbled Dad.

"You'd better wake up," I told him. There's burglars and they're in the keeping room.

That woke him up all right.

Willie crawled out from under the bed and began growling.

Dad headed for the door and bumped into the boys.

"Somebody's in the house," said Ethan.

"It's burglars," I told them.

"Where are you going, Jack?"

"Downstairs. Come on, boys."

"Oh, no you don't." Mom jumped out of bed and stood in the doorway. "Call the police."

"Call the police?"

"Yes, Jack. If there's a burglar down there he probably has a gun. He'll shoot you all." Mom was getting hysterical. I was scared too.

Willie was trembling and trying to get back under the bed.

"Don't be silly." Dad pushed Mom aside. "I'm sure there's no one down there. We'll just check." He and the boys started toward the front stairs.

"I'm calling the police," Mom said in a loud whisper.

"Don't you dare," Dad whispered back twice as loud.

I figured Mom was safe with Willie, so I ran after Dad and the boys.

"Anybody there?" Dad called as we went creeping down the stairs.

The farther down we went, the darker it got.

"Ouch," said Jon. "You're on my foot, Kyle."

"I am not. Watch out, will you, Ethan?"

"It's not me, I'm still up here."

"Shh," said Dad as we all stumbled down the hallway toward the keeping room.

We could hear the voices clearly now. It sounded like gangsters fighting.

"I warned you before and I'm warning you now, don't play with guns, Louie."

"Yeah?"

"Yeah. Drop it, drop that gun."

Dad and the boys headed for the door. There was an explosion, like a machine gun. I screamed and grabbed Dad. He collided with the boys and we all fell on the floor.

Suddenly the guns stopped, and I heard someone snoring. It sounded like Dad. We got up and pushed the door open. Dad fumbled for the light. What do you know? There, right in front of us, lying on the braided rug, was the Library Media tape recorder. Sitting right next to it was that black cat.

We stood there, still out of breath and shaking. Meowner walked over to the sofa and jumped up onto the end table.

Ethan began hopping up and down. "I know what happened. It was the cat. The cat knocked the tape recorder off the end table."

"Sure," said Jon, "and when it fell on the floor, the jolt must have released the playback switch. It's really weird, B.J. The chances of that happening are a million to one."

"Did I hear shots?" Mom came running into the room carrying Jon's official B.B. gun. Willie tagged after her, hiding behind her nightgown.

"The burglar was Humphrey Bogart," I told her.

"What happened? What's the matter?" Allison came down the back stairs.

"There was a burglar," Kyle said. "And you slept through it all."

"No! Why didn't somebody wake me?"

"Yeah, and he ate the lemon pie," yelled Jon from the kitchen.

Willie spotted Meowner. He barked and dived under the table after her.

"What's that cat doing in the house?" Before Mom could grab Meowner and toss her out, we heard the sirens.

"It's the cops," yelled Ethan.

Everyone tried to beat each other out of the keeping room and up the front stairs. At the top, Dad stopped Mom.

"Oh, no you don't. You invited them, Dorothy. You entertain them." Then he turned to me. "And B.J. will help."

Mom put on her housecoat and marched downstairs.

I got my old bathrobe and went slowly down the back way.

Mom was talking to Chief Valenti and Sergeant Lewis.

"You mean, this is the burglar?" Meowner brushed against Sergeant Lewis.

"Black cat, bad luck!" laughed Chief Valenti.

"B.J. says it's good luck." Mom sure sounded sarcastic. Then she had to go and tell them all about me being gifted and a fortune-teller. It was really humiliating. Worst of all, I had to read their horoscopes while she served them coffee.

As they were leaving, Chief Valenti offered to take Meowner back with them to the police station. "Not to lock her up," he joked, "but we could use a good mouser."

"She's yours," said Mom.

Before I had a chance to protest, she picked up the cat by the back of the neck and handed her to Chief Valenti.

Mom and Meowner both began sneezing.

"They're allergic to each other," I said to Sergeant Lewis.

Fortunately Mom was too tired to give me a long lecture. She couldn't resist saying something, though. "Now do you realize how full of nonsense those books are, young lady? There's not a speck of truth in any one of them."

I didn't dare tell her it had all happened just as my books predicted. I was let down, disappointed, and I'd lost Meowner.

But what I couldn't understand was why my E.S.P. failed to warn me about being one of the chosen excerpts from the police blotter.

And wouldn't you think Nancy Tyler would be more loyal than to bring the newspaper to school and show it to that Tony Spano? He grabbed it from her and read it out loud to the whole class.

" 'Wednesday, two forty-five A.M.' " What a stupid, obnoxious voice! " 'Burglary report from Pinkerton residence on Viewland Drive. Investigation reveals burglar is tape recorder and black cat. Black cat apprehended and taken to police station.' "

So when Mr. Jakeman played the tape, I nearly died. The class laughed all the way through it — especially the part where I tell Mom about eggs being used as a protective spell. It sounded like "smell."

Goldilocks and
Number Twenty-Three

It was late November, almost time to pose for the Christmas card again. I could hardly believe it. I kept waiting for Mom to mention calling Mr. Buckingham about an appointment. Isn't it ridiculous? Everybody thinks it's ridiculous. That is, everybody except Mom. But in the beginning, she thought it was ridiculous too.

"I remember when your Mother and I were first married," Dad told me. "She received a Christmas card from an old classmate with a baby's picture on it. She nearly laughed her head off. 'Isn't that ridiculous?' she howled. As soon as she started having babies of her own, she'd worry half the year about how she was going to arrange all of you on the card. The other half of the year, she'd worry about what cute saying she could think of to go with it."

I thought I knew why Mom hadn't called Mr. Buckingham. It was the boys' long hair, especially Kyle's. It was her own fault. I mean, Mom and Dad have always believed in letting us express ourselves. So when Kyle let his hair grow last spring, nobody said much. Mom complained for a while that he never brushed it, and once she had to cut a knot out of it as big as a bird's nest, but we all got used to it.

I liked it. I told Kyle my fortune-telling book said there was a magic of strength and power in long hair, like in the Bible story of Samson and Delilah.

Jon and Ethan decided to let their hair grow too. By October, all the boys' hair was almost as long as Allison's and mine. In fact, from the back, when we were all wearing blue jeans, you could hardly tell who was who.

I figured Mom was embarrassed to send out Christmas cards to her old friends with the boys and all that hair. Or maybe Mom hadn't had time to call Mr. Buckingham because we were so busy Saturdays going to football games.

Kyle had made the high school varsity team. He's only a substitute, but Dad loves to go to all the games. We have to go too, if we're not busy. Mom says it's part of being a family, to do things like that together, even if Kyle never does get to play much.

We all wanted to go this Saturday, though. It was our final game, and we were about to become the champions of our county.

The bleachers were crowded. I got a seat with Mom and Dad on the home-team side. Allison and Amy Walker sat in front of us. Ethan and Jon had to stand down near the field. The bleachers on the visitor's side were filled. Coach Dodd and the team came running onto the field. The cheerleaders started jumping up and down. The team looked good. There was no doubt about it, we were going to win for sure.

Then Sleepy Hollow came running onto the field and I wasn't so sure. They were tremendous. They made our team look like Tony Spano's sixth-grade baseball team. I started to get nervous even before the referee blew the whistle for the kickoff.

Kyle was sitting on the bench. I spotted him right away, with his long blond hair coming out from under his helmet. It fell between his shoulder pads and practically covered the green number twenty-three on his shirt. That's a very unlucky number. I told Kyle he should ask Coach Dodd for another one. He ignored my suggestion. I even typed a paragraph from my *Tablet of Magic Numbers* and left a copy of it for him on his dresser.

> Twenty-three... this is a very precarious number and will bring many drastic changes in your life. You should consider all present activities and take the necessary measures to avoid problems. You may be "cut off" from a prized possession. Someone is out to get you.

Kyle still didn't pay any attention to my warning. I didn't have to worry though, Coach Dodd wouldn't dare use a substitute today. This game was going to be too close.

I was right. Those Sleepy Hollow players were not so sleepy. They scored two touchdowns in the first quarter. Then we tied them, 14–14, by half time. Nobody felt very comfortable.

The cheerleaders marched with Stratton Swane's band around the field singing the school song. I bumped into Nancy at the P.T.A hotdog stand. I was so excited I forgot to order one.

At the end of the third quarter, the other

team kicked a field goal and Sleepy Hollow led again, 17–14.

People were screaming and jumping all over the stands. I didn't see Fred Calganinni get knocked out, but there he was, lying flat on the field, our star field-goal kicker, and our only chance to at least tie the game.

Coach Dodd was motioning to Kyle. Kyle buckled his helmet and ran out onto the field.

"What's happening, Dad?"

"Kyle is Fred's substitute, B.J. The coach is sending Kyle in to try to tie up the game with a field goal. It's our fourth down on their twenty-yard line. It's the last quarter and we can't possibly get close enough to the goal to make a touchdown."

I wished I had some salt to throw over my left shoulder for luck.

"Now our quarterback is on his knees. The ball is being snapped back from the center to Quarterback Tom Cook." Dad sounded like a sports announcer on television. "Oh, no. Tom fumbled the ball. Kyle can't kick it. Instead, instead—"

"Instead he's picking it up," I screamed.

"He's running for a touchdown," Mom shouted.

And he was, with his hair flying behind him,

he was running with all the strength of Samson for a touchdown that would win the game and make us the county champions.

Above all the yelling I heard someone from the bleachers on the visiting team side. "There goes Goldilocks, isn't he pretty."

He meant Kyle. Then more joined in. "Yoohoo, Goldilocks, get Goldilocks."

Kyle turned his head toward the bleachers. He heard them.

"Get Goldilocks, get Goldilocks," the whole visiting crowd was screaming as Kyle ran toward the goalposts.

That made Kyle so mad he ran faster than ever, but one of the Sleepy Hollow players was right behind him.

"Run, Kyle, run," I screamed.

"He's on the ten-yard line," Dad yelled to Mom. "He's going to make it."

On the five-yard line the fellow behind Kyle reached out.

"Watch it, Kyle, watch it," I hollered.

It was too late. The player had grabbed Kyle's hair and pulled it. Kyle swayed. Another fellow flew at his feet and tackled him. Kyle fell on the three-yard line. The whistle blew. The game was over. I collapsed back on my bleacher seat. It was all the fault of that number twenty-three. Someone was out to get Kyle all right. And they did.

That evening, we were all at the table for dinner, except Kyle.

"Run upstairs and tell Kyle dinner's ready, B.J.," Mom said.

I was about to get up when Kyle came down the stairs.

Everybody just stared.

Allison finally blurted out, "Why Kyle, you cut your—"

I kicked her under the table. I could have cried. My Samson looked like a skinned cat. He looked dreadful. So that was the prized possession the number twenty-three said would be cut off! Kyle had taken the scissors and, with two snips, cut all his hair off. It was as though he held half in one hand and cut it, and then the other side, the same way. It went like an upside-down *V* in the back, but with one long piece in the middle he'd missed.

"You played a fine game, Kyle," Dad said to him. "I'm proud of you."

"Yes, you did." Mom sat down. Then quietly added, "I like your haircut. Perhaps you might get it shaped a bit at the barber's when Jon and Ethan get theirs cut for the Christmas card."

No one moved or spoke.

"Mom." Kyle stood up. "Mom, I'm not posing for the Christmas card anymore. I think it's silly. I'm too old for that."

I couldn't believe my ears. That was Kyle, and he was talking like a Samson. He was a Samson all right, and even without his long hair, he had more strength than ever before.

"Kyle's right, Mom," said Jon. "And I'm too old, too."

"So am I," added Ethan.

"Hooray," I whispered.

Allison sat there, looking disappointed.

Before Mom could reply, Dad spoke. "I guess that settles that. Let's eat."

The phone rang.

I jumped up to answer just to get away from the table. Mom looked so sad I was afraid Dad might change his mind.

Wouldn't you know? It was Mr. Buckingham.

"It's for you, Mom. Mr. Buckingham. He says it's getting late. If you want to have those Christmas cards ready in time, you'd better make an appointment."

"I'll make it now." Mom got up and took the phone.

As I sat down we heard her say, "Oh, yes, George. That's fine. Tuesday at noon." She hung up.

"We'll be in school Tuesday," Allison reminded her as she came back to the table.

"Didn't you tell Mr. Buckingham what we decided?" Dad sounded angry.

Mom sat down and put her arm around him. "Jack, I've been childish and unreasonable. I apologize to you all. And I promise I'll do something different for this year's card." She turned to Kyle. "Kyle, you should let your hair grow again. It looks better long. Now, who wants dessert?"

The Vision

It was two weeks before Christmas. The whole family was together in the keeping room, relaxing after dinner. I was lying on the braided rug in front of the fireplace with Willie.

"Holy Christopher! It's only five above outside," shouted Jon as he checked his thermometer through the picture window.

"Don't say that, Jon." Mom was addressing Christmas cards at the table.

"What, Mom?"

"Holy whatever. It's not right."

"How's this look?" Allison was standing on a

chair hanging fresh green boughs above the doorway.

Kyle sat down on the window seat to help Ethan open some cards that had arrived in the morning mail.

"Hey, everybody. Look at this!" Ethan jumped up and started dancing around. He was holding a large card over his head. Jon grabbed it out of his hand and started howling. Kyle tackled Jon and knocked Allison over. We were all grabbing the card and tumbling over the floor. Dad finally rescued it for Mom.

It was from the Spanos. It had all those kids grinning in front of their fireplace. Marianne was holding a rabbit by the ears, and so were Suzanne and Johnny and Joe. And did that Tony Spano ever look foolish standing there with his baseball cap on backward.

"Now—isn't that ridiculous, Mom?" I asked.

Mom looked down at me and winked.

"I guess we're all ridiculous some time or other, B.J.," Dad said.

Suddenly I wanted to hug them. So I did. I jumped up and hugged them both real hard.

That's when it came to me — the Vision. *I* was ridiculous, too, thinking I was gifted with all that magic and horoscopes and stuff. My family knew I was acting ridiculous all the time, but they went along with me, like we had gone along with Mom and the Christmas cards.

I stood there, like a dummy, looking at them all. So what if I wasn't gifted? So what if I didn't have a musical talent like Kyle, or wasn't a student like Jon, or couldn't catch skunks like Ethan, or ride a horse like Allison? I was happy just to belong to the Pinkerton family.

The only thing was—Nancy. I hated to hurt her feelings but I decided I'd better phone her right away and get it over with.

"You see, Nancy," I explained. "I'm not gifted. It was only a phase I was going through, like Mom and the Christmas cards."

"What?"

"Only it didn't take me as long to grow out of it."

"Well, don't worry, B.J. Why don't you become a model instead? I saw this ad in the paper and we can become models by going to this school."

"I'll have to think about it, Nancy."

I ran back to the keeping room.

"Guess what, everybody? Nancy Tyler's going to be a model."

"She's got long legs, anyway," said Kyle.

I ran upstairs. What a relief! I wasn't a fortune-teller anymore! I took my crystal ball out of the secret hiding place and put it on my bureau. Maybe I could drill a hole in it and make a vase for Mom. Then I took all those books off the shelf and stacked them in a corner in my closet. I could give them to Marianne. They would make a good Christmas gift.

As I climbed into my pajamas, the phone rang. It's Uncle Dave calling long-distance, I thought. I ran out of my room and stood listening at the top of the back stairs. It was Uncle Dave all right. That Uncle Dave, he always calls just before Christmas.

I leaned over the banister and yelled, "Good night, everybody."

Back in my room, I snuggled down in my bed and pulled the blankets up around me. Well, I thought, I certainly didn't want to be a model like Nancy, but there were lots of other things I could do. I could take piano or guitar lessons, or better still, I could do something worthwhile. Maybe I could join in the fight to save the dolphins, or have a garage sale and raise money to help people all over the world, or...

I felt something under my pillow. It was my horoscope book. I'd forgotten to check it! "As the year closes, the major planets are in favorable aspect to your sign." I read on. "Opportunities for your next undertaking will greatly improve. Nothing can stop you. You will be successful in anything you attempt."

I closed my eyes. What do you know? For a moment I thought my magic circle was completely surrounding me, but only for a moment, because then I fell asleep.

A Christmas Card

That's Willie, sitting in his old chair with a red ribbon tied around his collar. The thing that looks like it's growing out of the table is a topiary tree that Mom made in Mrs. Watson's Holiday Potpourri class. That's Willie's diploma leaning against it. You'd never know Mom patched the armchair for the picture, because while Mr. Buckingham was setting up his equipment, the phone rang and Willie's earmuffs fell off. You can't see them because they're on the floor. Willie got nervous and started chewing up the chair. Can you see the piece of cotton stuffing on his nose? Mom says she thinks Willie looks so cute smiling that way. I don't think he's smiling. I think he looks that way because he's about to bite Mr. Buckingham.

MERRY CHRISTMAS
The Pinkertons

About the Author

Pat Kibbe graduated from the American Academy of Dramatic Arts, and besides Broadway, television, and radio shows to her credit, she has also done commercials for Perdue Chickens and Ruffles Potato Chips. For her books, she draws from her own life. The Pinkerton family in *The Hocus-Pocus Dilemma* bears a strong resemblance to her own husband, dog, and five children (now grown). Currently, Pat Kibbe and her husband live in Yorktown Heights, N.Y. Her second book, *My Mother the Mayor, Maybe* is also available in an Apple Paperback edition from Scholastic, Inc.